"You don't have a second name?" the scarred man—Ares—asked, the first words he'd said personally to her since the ceremony.

"No," she said. "Perhaps I had one once, but I can't remember what it was. I'm just Rose."

What he thought of that, she had no idea, since he betrayed no reaction to the news whatsoever.

A few minutes later, a copy of the document was given to her.

"Here," said Ares. "Your marriage certificate."

Rose looked down and saw her own name. *Rose Aristiades.*

It gave her a little jolt. For years and years, she'd had no last name. For years and years, she'd only been Rose. But now she wasn't. She had a last name now and a connection to someone.

She had a husband.

She looked up at him, but he'd already turned away, heading toward the door. He paused in the doorway and glanced back at her, enigmatic as a sphinx. "I will see you in three months, Rose."

Then he was gone.

Jackie Ashenden writes dark, emotional stories with alpha heroes who've just gotten the world to their liking only to have it blown apart by their kick-ass heroines. She lives in Auckland, New Zealand, with her husband, the inimitable Dr. Jax, two kids and two rats. When she's not torturing alpha males and their gutsy heroines, she can be found drinking chocolate martinis, reading anything she can lay her hands on, wasting time on social media or being forced to go mountain biking with her husband. To keep up-to-date with Jackie's new releases and other news, sign up to her newsletter at jackieashenden.com.

Books by Jackie Ashenden

Harlequin Presents

The World's Most Notorious Greek
The Innocent Carrying His Legacy
The Wedding Night They Never Had
The Innocent's One-Night Proposal

Pregnant Princesses

Pregnant by the Wrong Prince

Rival Billionaire Tycoons

A Diamond for My Forbidden Bride
Stolen for My Spanish Scandal

Visit the Author Profile page
at Harlequin.com for more titles.

Jackie Ashenden

THE MAID THE GREEK MARRIED

HARLEQUIN
PRESENTS

HARLEQUIN®
PRESENTS™

Recycling programs
for this product may
not exist in your area.

ISBN-13: 978-1-335-58396-3

The Maid the Greek Married

Copyright © 2022 by Jackie Ashenden

For questions and comments about the quality of this book,
please contact us at CustomerService@Harlequin.com.

Harlequin Enterprises ULC
22 Adelaide St. West, 41st Floor
Toronto, Ontario M5H 4E3, Canada
www.Harlequin.com

Printed in U.S.A.

THE MAID THE GREEK MARRIED

CHAPTER ONE

Spring

THE LITTLE MAID was cleaning his room again.

Ares had come in to prepare for drinks with his father-in-law and there she was, on her knees in front of the big stone fireplace, sweeping ash out of the grate, and humming.

And she kept on humming as he shut the door behind him and strolled across to the chair that stood near the fireplace and sat down.

She kept on humming as if he wasn't even in the room.

He'd thought that humming would irritate him the first time she'd appeared to clear the fireplace, but it didn't. He even liked it. The soft sound of her voice was light, with a pleasing husk to it. Feminine. Soothing.

Mainly, though, he liked that she hummed as if he wasn't Ares Aristiades, CEO of Hercules Security, one of the largest private security companies on the planet and in demand from governments the world over.

Ares Aristiades, ex–French Foreign Legion, scarred and broken and harder than the Greek mountains he'd been born in.

Ares Aristiades, whose heart and soul had died years ago, and now was burdened with neither.

Duty, though, remained, because here he was, visiting his in-laws at their remote mountain compound near the Black Sea. The way he'd done most years since Naya had died. Or at least, the years he hadn't been either in hospital or in the Legion.

This particular maid had cleaned his room every year for the past five years, though it had only been in the last two years that he'd noticed her humming. And the last year he'd become aware that she was a woman and that the plain black dress she wore did nothing to hide the lush curves of a nineteen-fifties pinup.

She had long, honey-gold hair that she kept pinned in a severe bun at the nape of her neck and a sweet, heart-shaped face. Her mouth was full, her nose slightly tilted, her lashes long and looked like they'd been dipped in gold.

The staff here weren't permitted to meet the eyes of the guests, or so his father-in-law had said—a strange rule for staff that Ares didn't see the point of but hadn't been interested enough to argue about—and the little maid never had.

Apart from once, the previous year, as she'd scurried out of his room with her bucket full of ash. Those gold-dipped lashes had risen, and she'd flashed him a wide-eyed glance.

Her eyes had been golden too.

She'd only given him the briefest of looks before hurrying away, but there had been no fear in them, only a kind of awed curiosity.

Which was surprising. That wasn't people's usual response to him. People were usually… disturbed if not downright terrified. Facial scars had that effect, he'd discovered.

He'd thought she wouldn't be back cleaning his room after that, yet here she was, a year later, kneeling in front of the fireplace, once more shovelling ash.

He didn't know what to make of it.

He didn't know what to make of the desire that had ignited the moment her golden eyes had met his. He'd thought that as dead and gone as his wife, but one look from the little maid and it had roared into life, as raw and as powerful as it had been when he'd been young.

He didn't know why he still felt it even though a year had passed since that one brief glance, yet he did.

What was different about this woman, he

wasn't sure, nor did he care to think about it in any depth. But it had made him aware that the years were passing, and he wasn't getting any younger. And that he'd made certain promises.

Promises to his father that he wouldn't let the blood of Aristiades die with him.

Promises to his late wife that they would fill their house with children.

Both his father and his wife were gone, but those promises were iron chains, and he couldn't—wouldn't—break them.

His conscience had died with his wife and now all that kept him on the right path was her memory and the promises they'd made to each other.

His father, Niko, had been very insistent that the line of Aristiades must be preserved, especially since they were descended from the mighty hero Hercules. And although Ares had no use for bloodlines himself and it didn't matter to him if he was the last Aristiades, he'd sworn to his father he'd preserve it.

But it was for Naya's memory that he'd actually do it. She'd always loved children and they'd planned on a big family, and even though she was gone, those plans hadn't changed. His entire life since she'd died had been about honouring her, and having children would be another thread to add to that complex tapestry.

However, if he wanted them, he was also going to need a wife, and really, the sooner the better.

The room set aside for him was stone, its hard lines made softer with expensive silk rugs on the floor and velvet curtains. Not that he cared for rugs or curtains or anything that could be termed 'soft.'

Yet this little maid looked soft, and he liked that more than he'd anticipated.

'What is your name?' he asked in Russian, assuming she was Russian since she worked here. His voice sounded rusty and harsh, cutting through the silence like a rockfall in a quiet valley, but he took no notice. His vocal cords had been damaged in the fire and he was long used to that by now.

She gave a start. 'Rose,' she said in her light, husky voice. Then she turned her head and looked at him over her shoulder. 'What's yours?'

Her eyes were exactly as he remembered from a year earlier, like big golden coins, and once again there was no horror in them. No pity, either, or even compassion for the massive burn scars that pulled at his skin. She looked at him as if she didn't see his scars at all.

Such pretty eyes.

The raw flicker of desire burned brighter, higher, yet he made no move. He wasn't a boy at the mercy of his passions any longer, no matter how unfamiliar those passions might be these days. He was a man in complete control of himself. A man who could be patient when the situation demanded it.

A man who didn't hide the scars that ravaged his face, a continual reminder of the dangers of pride.

He didn't care what she thought of them. He didn't care what anyone thought of them. They were no one's business but his.

He stared back, letting her look. 'You do not know?'

Her gaze never wavered. 'No. I'm not told the names of our guests.'

Ares was due downstairs in five minutes, and it wasn't appropriate to engage a servant in idle conversation, but Ivan, his father-in-law, could wait.

Ivan was a Russian oligarch with too many fingers in too many pies, and had never forgiven Ares for how his daughter had fallen in love with a lowly Greek shepherd boy while holidaying in Athens. Ivan had objected to the marriage, but Naya had always been a strong woman and she'd wanted Ares. She'd never cared that he lived in a hut in the mountains without a drachma to his name.

Over the years, Ares had increased in Ivan's

estimation after he'd left the hut behind and become who he was, the God of War, as he was known in some circles.

Ares didn't like Ivan, though. Not that he was here for Ivan. He was here because Naya would have wanted him to be and so here he was.

'Why do you want to know?' he asked, deciding he wouldn't give it to her yet. She was only a maid, though he had to admit, she didn't much act like one.

She didn't answer immediately, a small crease appearing between her golden brows. Then she dumped the shovel full of ash, and the brush, and turned around to face him. She stood up, ash dusting her uniform, but she didn't brush it away. In fact, she didn't seem to notice it at all.

Her expression had taken on a set look, as if she was steeling herself for something. 'I...need your help,' she said.

Ares stared at her, conscious of an unfamiliar feeling spreading through him. And it took him a couple of moments to realise that what he was feeling was surprise.

It had been a very long time since someone had surprised him, when these days he felt nothing at all. Not even a flicker of an emotion. So it was odd that one little maid should be able to coax it from him.

His legs were outstretched and crossed at the

ankle, the black leather of his shoes—handmade by a shoemaker in Milan—glossy in the evening sun coming through the window. She was standing just shy of his feet. Close, even.

Close for a little maid with seemingly no fear of the man who was sitting bare inches away. A man worth billions who had governments in his pocket.

A man who was scarred, yet still physically powerful and who could crush her without effort.

A man she apparently thought could help her.

Ares was not accustomed to being asked for help and he was even less accustomed to giving it.

'Help,' he echoed, tasting the word. 'You think *I* could help you.'

'Yes.' She didn't seem to notice that he hadn't made it a question. 'I have no one else.'

If she was coming to him, then she must indeed have no one else.

He tilted his head back slightly, studying her.

She wasn't tall. In fact, even standing while he was sitting, she was barely at eye level. But there was a determination to her, a stubbornness, he could see it in the cast of her chin. Her gaze met his unflinchingly, though he could see the hint of desperation to it.

Her black dress did her no favours, but it

didn't hide the lush promise of those curves either. She had a sweet, womanly figure, which was really all he required in a wife, though why he was thinking that this little maid shovelling ash could fit the bill he had no idea.

Then again, why not? It didn't matter which woman he chose, she'd never be Naya, and that meant one pretty woman was as good as any other. She clearly wasn't bothered by his scars, though, which was a considerable point in her favour. He didn't care what people thought of them, yet he also didn't want to be confronted by distaste or fear over the breakfast table every morning. Or in his bed every night.

'Well?' she asked. Her hands had curled into fists at her sides, though her small, delicate features were unreadable.

A woman used to hiding what she felt, he suspected.

'Help with what?' He really shouldn't be continuing with this conversation, considering Ivan, but now he was curious and more than happy for his father-in-law to have to wait.

Rose stared with a direct, unblinking gaze. It might have been disconcerting for a lesser man, but Ares had never been, nor would he ever be, a lesser man.

Her lovely mouth compressed, and she shifted on her feet at last. Nervous, obviously. Then she darted a gaze at the door, as if she was worried about eavesdroppers. 'They're going to sell me,' she said, the words falling over themselves in their efforts to escape. 'Tomorrow, I think, or maybe the day after, I'm not sure. I don't know where I'll be going or to who, but I don't want to stay to find out. I need to escape somehow, but I've got no money and I've never been out of this compound, and I can't get out of here anyway, not without help, and I know because I've tried. Someone has to get me out and I have no one else to ask.' She took a shuddering breath. 'Please, sir. Please, help me.'

Rose knew she'd said too much the moment the words were out of her mouth. They'd escaped as if he'd somehow tripped a switch inside her, causing all her desperate fears to come cascading out.

She didn't want to sound like a scared little girl. Scared little girls were victims and she was tired of being a victim. She'd been one for her entire life and that had to stop. Here. Now. Today.

The man said nothing, sprawled out in the seat in front of her as if he didn't have one single care in the entire world. Because of course he didn't. Men like him never did. The rich, the powerful, the infamous. All kinds stayed at the compound, and she'd seen them all. She was a house servant, and it was her job to make their beds and clean their fireplaces, scrub their baths and pick up their clothing.

Some were terrible, lashing out with a cuff for no reason at all, and others groped her because she was there, and they thought they had the right. Some shouted at her for some imagined slight, and some made disgusting insinuations, then laughed. Some ignored her like she wasn't even there.

But this man… This man was different, and he always had been.

Rose stared fixedly at him.

He was immensely tall, immensely powerful. Built broad and muscular like the guards that kept watch over the doors of the compound. Except for all their physical strength, the guards seemed small and insubstantial next to this man. They thought they were wolves and maybe they were, but this man was a dragon.

He projected the strength of a giant, the arrogance of a king and the confidence of God himself, and she had no idea who he was that granted him such massive self-assurance, but one thing she was sure of: he could help her.

She'd been cleaning this room for five years and it was only the previous year that she'd risked punishment by looking at him. She already knew he was tall and that his voice was cracked and broken sounding. That he walked silently and with a grace that was almost shocking in a man built so broad.

His scars had been shocking too, but only because she hadn't expected them.

She didn't care about his scars. The only thing she cared about was that he was the only one who didn't paw at her, who didn't try to touch her, or say disgusting things and make crude jokes whenever she was in the room. He didn't shout at her or even make conversation.

He wasn't one of those men who ignored her either, though.

She'd sensed him watching her, and why he did so, she wasn't sure, but it didn't frighten her. His attention felt curious rather than threatening, though again, she wasn't sure why that was. Perhaps it was her humming. Perhaps he liked it.

That was beside the point, though. What mattered was that he'd never made a single move towards her, not one. It didn't mean he was any better than all the rest, but it was a sign that he was at least no worse, and that was as good as she could get in a place like this.

Not that she had a choice now. They were going to sell her tomorrow and he was her only chance of escape.

She stared at him without blinking, willing him to say something, her heart thudding uncomfortably loudly in her ears.

He stared back, in no hurry. As if he hadn't even heard her little speech.

She swallowed, a feeling she didn't understand flickering like a fire inside her.

He wore an exceptionally well-cut suit of dark grey wool; she knew a good tailor when she saw one, she was nothing if not observant. His shirt was snowy white and open at the neck—he hadn't bothered with a tie.

She found herself uncomfortably mesmerised by the glimpse of his throat, though she couldn't imagine why. His skin was dark bronze, the white of his shirt showing it off to good effect, and his hair was darkest black and cut close to his skull. His eyes were startling, a strange silvery green, like a tarnished sea.

He was a man wrought of iron, everything about him hard. Yet there were great gouges in his face, scar tissue twisting one side of it, while leaving the other side almost unmarked. That side was beautiful, high cheekbones, beautiful mouth, straight nose, while the other side was… scar tissue and melted flesh.

Horrifying. Compelling. Frightening. Magnetic.

She couldn't settle on which, but that didn't

matter either. She needed his help and she needed it now.

'Who is going to sell you?' His voice was deep and harsh. It sounded like stones scraping over one another.

'The boss,' she said. 'Ivan Vasiliev.'

The man's expression was merely one of polite interest, though it was difficult to tell with those horrific scars clawing his face. He certainly didn't seem worried or upset or even angry as she'd mentioned Vasiliev's name.

Perhaps he knew that Ivan Vasiliev had bought two children through human trafficking networks, and that one had been chosen to be his daughter, while the other had ended up as a servant. Perhaps it didn't bother him. Perhaps he'd even been involved with it himself.

Rose went cold at that thought, but she let none of her fear show. Hiding her emotions was one of the first things she'd learned how to do when she'd arrived here and now it was so ingrained it was automatic.

It didn't matter if he was involved. The only thing that mattered was that he could get her out. Athena had told her she was going to be sold and Rose believed her implicitly. But Athena hadn't known details such as why or to who, but neither of them ever knew those things.

Rose had been brought here as a child, given

the bare minimum of schooling, then put to work. She'd never been allowed to leave, not even once, and all forms of communication with the outside world were banned. All she knew was what she'd managed to glean from eavesdropping on conversations and discussions with Athena.

There had been moments over the years where she'd thought about trying to escape, but the practicalities had always defeated her, and so she'd stayed. Yet she'd never forgotten that she was a prisoner.

And now Vasiliev was going to get rid of her, she wasn't even that. She was property.

'I see,' the man said in his rough, scraping voice, the expression on his scarred face impassive. 'And what makes you think I'll help you, Rose?'

'I don't think you'll help me,' she answered bluntly. 'I only hope that you will.'

He was silent a moment, the intensity of his silvery-green gaze unnerving. 'Why me?'

Rose clenched her hands unconsciously. 'I have no one else to ask. There are no other guests and… You are the only one who hasn't tried to touch me. Not once.'

He gave a grating, mirthless laugh. 'That's all? Your bar for trustworthiness is very low.'

Rose ignored the tension coiling deep in her

gut. She had to convince him to help her, she had to. He was her last chance. 'I don't need to trust you. I just need you to get me out of here.' She took a steadying breath. 'I'll do anything you want. Anything at all.' She hadn't meant to offer herself, but she would. If it meant getting out of here, she'd let him do whatever he wanted with her. Athena had protected her from most unwanted attention—unlike some of the other women who did the cleaning—and so she hadn't been touched. But that didn't mean she didn't know what men wanted from a woman.

'Anything at all,' the man echoed softly and there was something in his voice that made her shiver, though she wasn't sure what it was. It wasn't an unpleasant shiver either. Strange. His gaze was very steady, not dropping to assess her figure the way some men's did. He stared right into her eyes.

Rose wasn't used to anyone seeing her, really *seeing* her. And not merely as a method by which a fireplace got clean or a bed got made, or as an object to either manhandle or beat. A thing. But seeing her as a person.

She wasn't sure she liked it. It made her insides shift uncomfortably, as if it was a challenge he was issuing and a part of her wanted to answer it. But that was difficult when the impact of his attention felt like a weight slowly pushing her into the floor.

His eyes are beautiful.

She gritted her teeth. She had no idea why she was thinking about his eyes, but she knew she couldn't look away. That would betray fear and betraying fear was just about the worst thing she could do. Fear invited beatings or worse. Strength was all in this place and so strength she would give him.

'So, you would give me your body if I asked for it?' His tone was very casual, as if he asked such things of women every day and with the same unblinking stare. 'Take off your uniform and lay yourself out naked on my bed?'

This is a test.

She didn't know how she knew; she just did. Just as she was clear she would pass it. She'd had such tests before and she'd never failed them.

'Yes,' she said. And then, because she wasn't the only one who could be tested, she added, 'Though you'll have to help me with the zip.' And she turned around, presenting her back to him.

Silence fell.

Her heartbeat thudded in her ears. Her awareness narrowed on him behind her, waiting for the sounds of him rising and coming over to her, taking the tab of her zip and pulling it down.

Her skin prickled.

She hoped he would be gentle, though he didn't look like a man who knew what gentleness was. Perhaps he would be quick then. Quick was good, or so she'd heard from the other maids.

Thank God Athena's protection had saved her from that. Athena had been brought here at the same time as she had, two little girls terrified out of their minds and clinging to each other during the long journey to Vasiliev's house. Athena too had been taken off the streets. Except Athena hadn't been chosen for servitude, she'd been chosen by Vasiliev's wife as a replacement for a daughter who'd died.

She now lived a life of pampered luxury, yet she was as much a prisoner as Rose. It was Athena who insisted Rose spend time with her, even though Vasiliev's wife disapproved. And it was Athena who'd let it be known that no one was allowed to touch Rose or else she'd be distraught, and no one wanted Athena distraught because that made Vasiliev's wife distraught, and Vasiliev would do anything for his wife.

Yes, Rose had been lucky. Rose had been protected. But no one would know if one of Vasiliev's guests decided to avail himself of her.

And it would be her word against his, the word of a woman absolutely no one cared about except Athena.

Rose stared at the dusty stone fireplace she'd just cleaned, everything inside her drawn tight. Her jaw ached. Yet still there was silence from behind her.

'The zip,' she said at last, impatient and wanting this to be over. 'I can't do it on my—'

'Your body doesn't interest me, little maid.' The words were heavy as falling boulders and she was shocked to feel a small sting. As if she was disappointed, which surely couldn't be true. She couldn't *want* him to touch her.

She turned around sharply. He was still sitting there in the chair, having not moved a muscle, his stare as unyielding as stone.

'I will pay you,' she said, desperation tightening in her gut. 'I don't have any money, but once I'm free, I'll get a job and I can—'

'I don't require your money either.' He tilted his head like a bird of prey, his gaze speculative in a way that made her shiver yet again. 'But I also do not do anything for free.'

'So, what do you want?' Her tone was too sharp, the words too blunt, and she knew she was behaving in a way that would normally earn her a punishment. Servants were expected to be invisible, and she'd learned that lesson early on. But she didn't take it back.

'I will need to think on it.' He glanced down at the chunky platinum watch that circled one strong wrist. 'But we can discuss that later. I have an appointment that I am now late for.'

Rose took a silent, shaking breath, her hands clenched into unconscious fists. Hope was dangerous and yet hope was all she had, and she had to know now. 'Does this mean you'll help me?'

He looked up from his watch, his silvery-green gaze enigmatic in the fading evening light. 'Yes,' he said. 'Why not?'

CHAPTER TWO

ARES STARED DOWN at the vodka he was holding, the cut crystal tumbler beaded with condensation. It was good vodka, clean and sharp—Ivan always had good vodka—but Ares found he'd lost his taste for it.

Ivan had poured him a drink and had immediately started into a business discussion that Ares had tuned out. Lately, his father-in-law had started trying to impress him with details of various dealings that Ares had no interest in. Ivan was angling to be a Hercules client, Ares knew. He wanted the highly trained black ops soldiers for his own security staff and the technology that was a Hercules specialty. He'd also mentioned that he had 'capital' and was looking for somewhere to invest it, and maybe he could invest in Hercules.

Ares didn't need any more investment and even if he did the last person he'd get it from was his father-in-law. He didn't want his father-in-law as a client either.

They were in Ivan's private study, and Ivan was standing at the huge fireplace, one elbow on the mantelpiece, his other hand holding a tumbler full of vodka.

He was a tall man and broad, and even in his early seventies, he still radiated the kind of cold power that was common in this part of the world. Power that came from money and the relentless selfishness that all men carried in their hearts.

Ivan was still talking about business opportunities, but Ares wasn't listening. His thoughts kept drifting back to the little maid and what she'd told him back up in his room. About being bought and then sold and how she needed help.

Ares knew that something had broken in him the night he'd tried to save his wife and failed. The beam that had fallen on him, pinning him in place and scouring away a good many of the nerves in his face, had also burned away the ability to feel any kind of emotion. His facial expressions were frozen as was some core part of him, and while some feeling had returned to his face over the years, the part of him that was frozen had remained so.

So, it was strange to find himself…almost on the verge of anger by what the little maid had told him. That Ivan had not only bought her but sold her too. Not that he was particularly surprised about that—Ivan had always been extremely morally grey.

Naya would have been appalled that her own father had been involved in such a thing, and she'd probably demand that something must be done.

That was why Ares had set up Hercules, a security company that went into places governments couldn't risk open involvement in, to fight for people who had no one to fight for them. To protect those who couldn't protect themselves and to even the odds against tyrants. He also provided services to countries who needed help during times of natural disasters or other such catastrophes.

Hercules was Naya's memorial and meant every contract he took on had to be something she would have approved of.

The little maid reminded him somewhat of Naya.

She'd stood in front of him, small and determined, every part of her lush figure set in stubborn lines, as if she'd fight the entire world for what she wanted.

She hadn't been afraid of him—or if she had been, she'd hidden it well—meeting his gaze without hesitation. And when she'd offered herself as payment and he'd called her bluff, she'd turned around, clearly ready to pay up.

He'd been surprised by the kick of lust that had provoked too, though perhaps that had merely been the long years of celibacy speaking. Then again, it wasn't as if he had a shortage of beautiful women all vying for his bed, and none of them had sparked anything inside him, not the way she had done.

Those women aren't warriors. The little maid is.

It was true. Perhaps that was why he'd agreed to help her in the end. Because he'd seen the ember of a warrior in every fierce line of her and he respected that. There was something… admirable in people who were willing to risk everything to get what they wanted, even when they were afraid. Even when they were desperate, and she was; he'd heard it in her voice.

But also, he'd agreed to help her because it was something Naya would have wanted him to do. Most especially when it was Naya's father who'd bought her in the first place.

Naya wouldn't have wanted you to require payment, though.

Ares stared down at his vodka, Ivan's voice a low drone in the background.

No, she would have wanted him to help Rose without requiring anything in return. Especially when Rose probably had nothing whatsoever to give him.

Ares swirled the vodka around in his tumbler, frowning at it, conscious that the unfamiliar feeling of anger collecting in his gut was getting stronger.

Anger at Ivan and the audacity of the man for sullying the memory of his daughter by buying and selling a young woman. He only had Rose's word for it that Ivan had bought her, but there was no question in Ares's mind that she'd been telling the truth. There had been nothing fake about the desperation in her eyes.

So, while his unexpected emotional response was disconcerting to say the least, there was no other option but to help her, regardless of whether she could pay him or not. Naya's memory commanded it.

It wasn't personal. He wouldn't do it because she'd touched him emotionally in any way, or because of that inconvenient spark of desire she'd ignited. He was dead inside, and nothing could reach him, least of all one little maid.

But Naya had been his conscience for years now and she was as ever his guide.

He would help the little maid for her, because she would tell him it was the right thing to do.

The little maid would make a good wife, though.

Ares's thoughts drifted.

Oh, she would, that was true. She was clearly a woman with backbone and the first to spark his interest sexually in years, and he suspected she was also fierce. She didn't seem to be afraid of his scars, or him either.

If he married her, he also wouldn't have to go through the tiresome process of finding a suitable woman elsewhere. He could, of course, but he didn't want to devote any time or energy to what was a relatively minor issue.

And although they hadn't exchanged a word with each other before today, he felt as if he almost…knew her. He'd watched her for two years now, going about the task of cleaning with such focused intensity it was as if she was heading into battle.

Would her approach to pleasure be like that too?

Ares dismissed the thought almost as soon as it had entered his head. It was an extremely inappropriate one to have about an imprisoned woman. Naya would not only be disappointed, she'd be appalled.

'Are you listening, Ares?' Ivan asked sharply.

'No,' Ares said without looking up from his vodka. 'How much do you want for the little maid?'

There was a shocked silence.

Ares lifted his gaze from his tumbler.

Ivan was giving him a narrow look. 'What little maid?'

'The one who cleans out the fireplace in my room every year when I visit. Blonde. She said her name was Rose.'

A strange ripple of expression crossed Ivan's craggy face. 'What do you mean how much—'

'I know you bought her, Ivan, don't bother pretending you didn't. So how much for her?'

He didn't want to get into a discussion about where Ivan had got her, or why. What was important now was getting Rose away as quickly as possible.

Ivan's mouth worked but nothing came out. Then he looked down at his tumbler abruptly and took a healthy swallow. 'I already have a buyer for her.'

No, indeed. The little maid had not been lying.

Ares swirled his vodka in a leisurely movement, betraying nothing of his thoughts. He might have told himself that rescuing Rose wasn't personal, but his anger certainly was, which surprised him and not in a good way. He'd thought his emotions dead and gone and quite frankly he preferred them that way. It did make things simple and he liked simple.

However, he sensed that nothing about this

situation was simple and now it was about to get even more complicated.

'Have you? Then I will double whatever has been offered for her.' Buying her wasn't ideal and he suspected Naya wouldn't like it, but it was the quickest way to get her out and with the minimum of fuss.

Ivan's gaze narrowed. 'What do you want with her?'

'Irrelevant. Do you want the money or not?'

'She is…very valuable,' Ivan said slowly. 'Athena likes her and whatever Athena wants, Athena gets, you know this.'

Athena was the Vasilievs' second daughter, spoiled and pampered as any princess. Ares didn't know her since she'd been adopted after Naya had died, but it was clear Ivan was only mentioning her because he'd sensed the resolution in Ares's tone and had decided that now was a good time to drive a hard bargain.

Ares's anger twisted inside him.

Ivan would be wrong.

'If she's so precious to Athena, then why are you selling her?' Ares asked idly.

Ivan took another swallow of his vodka, his gaze flickering. 'Athena is too attached, and the girl is a servant. Athena needs friends from her own social station.'

Ares wasn't interested in what Athena needed.

He was interested in Rose and whatever information he could get out of Ivan about her. 'And the girl? What can you tell me about her?'

Ivan shrugged. 'There's nothing to tell. She has no memory of anything before coming here. I don't know why. She was uninjured when she came to me, so it's not physical.'

A tightening sensation shifted behind Ares's breastbone. He ignored it. 'Nothing? What about family? Anyone who may potentially come looking for her?'

The older man shook his head. 'I have no idea. I don't go investigating the backgrounds of my servants. No one knows who she is and neither does she.'

She has no memories. She has no one. You know how that feels.

Well, he used to. Now, he felt nothing, though he suspected that wasn't the same for Rose. 'So Rose is not her name?'

'She couldn't remember her real name, so Athena gave her one.' Ivan frowned. 'I didn't intend to purchase her, that was a mistake. And I could have got rid of her, but I didn't. I kept her and gave her a safe home.'

This was clearly supposed to be admirable somehow, but Ares didn't find it a compelling argument. 'I don't care what you intended,' he said. 'It is of no interest to me. I will take the girl and I will take her tonight.'

Ivan's expression darkened. 'Tonight? But I haven't—'

'As I said,' Ares interrupted flatly. 'I will pay double for her. And if that is not to your liking, then I will pay you nothing and take her anyway.'

It wasn't something he would have chosen since he didn't relish getting one of his team in to storm his father-in-law's house, especially without going through the proper channels. He was meticulous about obeying the laws of whichever country his team happened to be in at the time. Then again, maybe he should storm the compound. Perhaps Ivan had bought other people that Ares didn't know about.

His father-in-law's expression had darkened still further. Ivan was not used to giving ground. Still, Ivan had never tested himself against Ares; mainly, Ares suspected, because he knew his son-in-law was more influential and far more powerful than he himself had ever been.

Ivan wouldn't let it come to that unfortunately. He knew he wouldn't win that battle, that diplomacy was the only way he could get what he wanted from Ares.

Pity. Ares hadn't had a decent battle for years. Still, Ivan would keep.

And sure enough, his father-in-law finally lifted a negligent shoulder. 'Very well, you may take her. But if you're leaving tonight, then there are some more important things I need to discuss with you.'

Ares was in no mood to discuss anything with Ivan. 'Not tonight,' he said curtly, before downing his vodka and rising to his feet. 'I've stayed too long as it is. As soon as the money is in your account, you will release her to me.'

He didn't wait for Ivan to respond, striding from the room and ignoring the older man's grumbling protest, filled with the sudden need not to spend any more time in the man's presence than he had to.

Ares organised the transferal of funds, gave a few orders regarding Ivan to one of his teams who specialised in financial investigation, then packed his bag.

It didn't take long, but it was full dark by the time he made his way to the compound's helipad.

The Hercules Security chopper was waiting for him, its rotors already spinning up as it prepared for take-off.

He ducked into the machine to find the little maid already tucked into the seat next to him with a headset on. She was still in her uniform and appeared to have no luggage about her person whatsoever, not even a handbag or purse. Her expression was steely, yet she was also pale, and he thought he could see fear glittering in her wide, golden eyes.

Once, he'd been the kind of man who'd taken his wife in his arms to comfort her after a nightmare. Who'd stroked her hair and told her he'd protect her from all harm. Once, he'd been a man who'd cared about such things.

But that man was dead and gone, along with his ability to provide comfort. He wasn't that man now and he never would be again.

So, all he said was, 'You have no belongings?'

She shook her head wordlessly.

She has nothing and no one.

Something tightened in his chest. He ignored it. 'No documentation?'

Another shake of her head.

'Do you have anywhere to go?'

Again, she shook her head.

Nothing. No one.

It wasn't a surprise. If Ivan had bought her as a child and she'd never left the compound, then of course she'd have nowhere to go.

He regarded her huddled in her seat, clutching at the leather, her jaw set in hard lines as if she was determined not to show her fear. But he could see it. She looked very small sitting there and very alone.

He rubbed at his chest absently, trying ease the unfamiliar ache that had settled there. 'So, what were your plans when you finally escaped?' he asked, because surely she must have had some idea about where she was going to go and what she would do.

She was silent a moment. 'I...thought I might go to Paris,' she said at last. 'I always wanted to go there.'

Paris. She wanted to visit Paris.

'And how were you going to get there?' A tugging sensation had joined the ache, along with the anger he'd felt just before in Ivan's study. 'With what money?'

She shook her head and glanced down at her lap.

No, she had nothing. No money, no documents. No belongings.

'What about family?' It came out sharp, but the anger hadn't gone away, and he didn't like it. He didn't even know why he was angry since she meant nothing to him. 'Do you have anyone you can contact?'

She kept her attention on her hands, every line of her tense. 'No. Or if I do, I don't remember them.'

No family either.

She truly was alone in the world.

Ares rubbed at his chest again, the ache persisting.

'I'm sorry.' She spoke so quietly he barely heard her. 'How did you... I mean, did you...' She paused yet again. 'Are you... Are you my owner now?'

The words made him feel as if there was a sullen fire burning behind his breastbone, outrage joining the heat of his anger.

'No,' he growled. 'I do not own people. I did have to pay Vasiliev money for you, but it was the quickest and easiest way to get you out. You are free, Rose.'

Her head lifted slowly, big golden eyes almost lost in the darkness. 'But you did have to buy me.'

The sullen fire burned higher. He ignored it. 'It was not my first choice. But freeing you by force would have taken some time.'

Her jaw hardened. 'I have no money, nothing to pay you back with—' She broke off suddenly, her expression tightening, fingers clutching at the seat as the helicopter shifted, lifting off the pad.

She was afraid, he could see that, but she was trying to hide it.

'There is nothing to fear,' he said, letting her know he saw it anyway. 'My pilot is the best in the business.'

Her gaze narrowed. 'I'm not afraid. It's only… I haven't been in a helicopter before.'

She might not have been in a helicopter before, but she was lying about not being afraid. Still, it was better that she be annoyed with him for pointing it out than giving in to her fear and cowering.

At the thought of her fear, the fire sitting in his chest burned brighter, hotter, the sensation so unfamiliar and alien that he couldn't process it. And he wasn't sure why he was feeling it now, when for years he'd felt nothing. He'd always sought Naya's memory for guidance about moral matters, yet now something inside him, an instinct he'd thought long dead, believed that what had happened to Rose was terrible and wrong, and she must be helped.

It was ridiculous. He couldn't understand what it was about her that should ignite any sensation in him at all. Perhaps it was merely physical, some by-product of desire.

'You will have to get used to it, since you are out now,' he said. 'If you want to go to Paris, I will take you—'

'As I was saying,' she interrupted suddenly. 'I have no money to pay you back now, but the moment I do, I swear I will.'

He stared at her. 'You don't have to pay me,

Rose.' Her name tasted oddly sweet on his tongue. 'You owe me nothing.'

'Yes,' she insisted. 'Yes, I do. You paid money for me.'

'And I have plenty of money. It was nothing.'

'It's not nothing.' There was an oddly determined look on her face. 'I know how things work. You don't get something for nothing. You paid for me and now I owe you a debt.'

The anger inside him kept on burning, scorching a hole in him. He didn't want it. He'd left his emotions in ashes on the floor of his burned-out house, and he was all the better for it. They weren't supposed to rise like a phoenix to haunt him again.

'You have no money,' he said curtly. 'Even if I did demand a price from you, exactly what are you supposed to pay me back with?'

She didn't look away. 'Well, what do you want?'

He didn't know why in the end he said it. But say it he did. 'What do I want? What I want, Rose, is a wife.'

Rose had prepared herself for the scarred man to want any number of awful things, but wanting a wife was not one of them.

She found herself staring at him in shock.

The unfamiliar movement of the helicopter

and the dull, rhythmic sound of the rotors were almost overwhelming even with the headset on, and she was overwhelmed enough as it was.

First, one of the house thugs had come to find her and had dragged her roughly outside. Naturally, she'd been anticipating a beating. Perhaps the scarred man had complained about her behaviour to Vasiliev and now she would be punished for her temerity.

Except she hadn't been punished.

She'd been dragged to the helicopter sitting on the helipad instead, and pushed inside it, a headset jammed on her head.

Nothing had been explained to her, but she was used to being in the dark about everything. She'd sat there, fighting fear, thinking that she was being taken to her new owner already and wondering whether there was any point to leaping out and running. At the same time, she also knew that no, there was no point, not when she had nowhere to run to.

Then, just as despair had set in, an immensely tall, broad figure had appeared from out of the house, illuminated by the outside lights and striding towards the helicopter.

There was no mistaking him. The scarred man. And she knew in that moment that he hadn't lied. He'd promised to get her out and he had.

A thousand questions had tumbled through her head, but then he'd pulled open the door and got in beside her, and every single one of those questions had vanished as quickly as they'd come.

The interior of the helicopter had felt very small, as if it had shrunk somehow, and he was taking up all the room. Every part of him seemed big and hard, wide shoulders, broad chest and powerful thighs. And what room he didn't take up physically he filled with the sheer weight of his presence.

She felt flattened by the force of him and his stare as he'd turned to look at her, the lights from the outside turning his scars into deep crevasses and gouges. Frightening and yet there was a strange beauty to him too. She didn't know how to process it.

She didn't know how to process her feelings either since there seemed to be many of them. Sharp relief that she was leaving. Terror at having to face a world she had only read about, never visited. Regret that she hadn't been given time to bring anything with her—not that she had anything anyway—or even say goodbye to anyone. Not that anyone would care except Athena. Excitement that she would finally see all those places she'd read about. Intense anxiety about what to do next.

Then he'd told her that he'd paid money for

her, and while it might have indeed been the quickest way to get her out, it now meant that she owed him. And while he might say that no, she owed him nothing, there was a debt there all the same. A string tying her to him, ensuring she'd never be completely free.

Or at least, not unless she paid him back.

He'd made it clear he wasn't after her body, and so she'd been prepared to offer him money—or at least future earnings from whatever job she'd managed to land. However, it seemed he didn't want money either.

Yet...a wife?

'Why?' she asked bluntly, since she might as well be blunt.

He lifted one massive shoulder. 'I require children. Time is passing and I have no heirs.'

You could use him.

The thought came out of nowhere, creeping through her brain and making her eye him warily. She had nothing and nowhere to go, not to mention only the vaguest idea of how the outside world even worked. There were identity documents such as birth certificates and passports and other things she would need, that she would have tremendous difficulty getting.

But he was clearly powerful, with 'plenty of money' or so he said, and while she trusted powerful, very rich men just about as far as she could throw them, which was not at all, he might be trustworthy enough to be of some use. He *had* been as good as his word and rescued her, after all, and perhaps he might even help further, with money and documents for example.

She already owed him for the money he'd paid for her, and if she asked for more help, she'd only owe him more. But if she gave him something he wanted, that could offset her debt. Something such as being his wife, for example. Which might even suit her purposes anyway since wives had power—certainly Vasiliev's did.

She lifted her chin and held his gaze. 'I could be your wife.'

If she'd shocked him, he didn't show it. 'You?'

The way he said the word, as if he couldn't conceive of a more ridiculous idea, stung unexpectedly and she found herself bridling. 'Yes, me. I know I'm not experienced in anything much except cleaning, but I'm a fast learner.'

'You did hear me when I said I wanted children?'

Rose wasn't deterred. She didn't have the first clue about what being a mother entailed but she wasn't inherently against the idea. In fact, she quite liked the thought of having a family, since she'd never known what it was to have one herself.

You know what that means, though, don't you?

Obviously. She'd have to have sex with him. Well, she'd been prepared to offer that before, hadn't she? It would be fine. She might be a virgin, but she knew all about sex. It had always sounded distasteful to her, but if what some of the others in the compound had told her was true, then it would be over in a few minutes.

It would be worth it if it meant she had freedom.

'I heard,' she said determinedly. 'I can give you children.'

His expression was impassive, yet something glittered in his silvery-green eyes. 'Are you bargaining with me, little maid?'

'I owe you,' she repeated, just so he was absolutely clear. 'But I also need money, a place to go and I'll definitely need documentation.'

'I can help you with those things. I do not require payment for them.'

'You might not, but *I* would still feel as if I owed you,' she pointed out. 'You need a wife who can give you children and I'm prepared to do that in return for all the help you can give me right now.'

He was silent a long moment, staring at her. 'Why?'

'Why marry you, you mean?'

'Yes. I've told you that you have no debt to me so why insist?'

'Because I don't want to feel as if I owe someone. The debt is still there even if you insist it isn't and I won't be truly free until I pay it.'

He said nothing, his expression giving nothing away.

'Well?' she asked.

'You really promise to give me children?'

'Yes. Millions of women do it. It can't be that hard.'

'Little maid,' he said, his voice just a touch too patient now. 'I don't think you fully understand what it is you're offering. Do you really think that having my child to repay a debt is a good idea?'

She flushed a little at that, because that was exactly what she'd been thinking, and opened her mouth to tell him that yes, it was a fine idea, when he went on, clearly not having finished, 'However, if this is something you feel you have to offer, then I have a counteroffer.' His eyes gleamed in the darkness. 'If I marry you so you can feel you have repaid part of your debt, I will insist that we not live together, nor will I claim my rights as a husband.'

Rose frowned. 'But that's not—'

'What I will require is that for the next year, you will spend two weeks of each season at my home so we can get to know one another.'

Rose's heart gave one loud beat that she heard even through the dull sounds of the rotors. 'Why? What's the point of that?'

'I don't think you understand what you are offering, little maid. I don't think you know what being a wife means, let alone being a mother. So, I will offer you the chance to find out.' His gaze was very direct and very compelling. 'If at the end of the year, having spent some time with me, you still wish to give me children, then we will remain married. If you do not, then I will have the marriage annulled and you may go on your way, your debt fulfilled.'

She bit her lip. It wasn't completely what she wanted, and it would mean feeling in debt to him for a whole year instead of getting the kid thing over and done with now. And it was strange that he should be the one with scruples about it. After all, she had no problems with being married to a stranger, so why should he?

Then again, she wouldn't have to live with him. She would have a year of complete freedom…

She almost couldn't imagine it. 'So,' she said slowly, wanting to be sure. 'I'll have a year on my own. To do…whatever I want? Go wherever I want?'

'Yes. I will arrange all the documentation you will need, including finances. I can also arrange for someone to help you set up a bank account, find a job, a place to live, all the things you'll need to start building a life for yourself.'

A little thrill of excitement went through her, the sensation so alien she almost didn't recognise it. A job. A place to live. A bank account. All the things that most people had, that she didn't, that meant she was actually going to have a proper life.

But it also meant more than that.

She hadn't told him the whole truth about her plans for when she escaped—she'd told no one, not even Athena. Never reveal anything, that was the key, that's what she'd learned over the long years in the compound. Be quiet and don't draw attention. Never give anyone anything that they might use against you, including your secrets. Never betray your emotions.

Yes, she had dreams of wanting to see Paris, but that wasn't the whole of it.

What she wanted was to find out who she was and where she came from, and maybe, one day, the family she'd been stolen from.

She'd told him she had no family, but the truth was, she really didn't know if she did or not. She had no memories at all of her life before being taken to the compound. There was only one thing she could remember and that was looking at some kittens in a shop window and someone saying, 'Wait here. I won't be long.'

Presumably that meant someone had been watching over her—a family member or a friend maybe—but she really had no idea who.

You might not have anyone.

That was a possibility. She might have been some street kid with no one, whom no one even knew she existed, but that thought was too depressing for words and so she tried not to think about it.

The main thing, though, if she wanted to find out who she was then she would need his help. She would need the money and documentation he offered, as well as someone to help her navigate her new life.

It seemed almost too good to be true.

Rose took a silent, steadying breath. 'You'd really do all of that for me?' she asked cautiously, not wanting to get her hopes up. 'And all you require is marriage?'

A strange half-smile twisted his mouth. 'I wouldn't say "all," Rose. Being my wife might not be easy for you.'

She wasn't sure what being a wife involved—if Vasiliev's wife was anything to go by, it seemed to involve a lot of shopping and lying around not doing terribly much—but it didn't sound like the worst thing in the world. How hard could it be? Maybe she'd even like it. Maybe at the end of a year, she'd want to stay married to him.

'Can't be any worse than my life in the compound,' she said.

Oddly, something that looked like amusement gleamed briefly in his eyes. 'I suppose that's true. But, Rose, you must be certain that this is what you want.'

'Of course I'm certain,' she said, and she was.

Perhaps she'd be able to navigate all of that on her own, perhaps she wouldn't; either way, things would be a lot easier with his help. And she was tired of having nothing. Tired of being a victim, of being prey. She never wanted to be prey again. And allying herself with this man would certainly ensure that wouldn't happen.

Being his wife was hardly a high price to pay. It was only for a year and she wouldn't even have to live with him.

His scarred and ruined face remained impassive. 'In that case, I accept your offer.'

Another strange little thrill coursed through her.

Are you sure this is a good idea? You don't know anything about him.

No, she didn't, but she was also short of options. And he hadn't forced her into anything. She'd offered herself to him and he'd declined. He'd even tried to decline her offer of payment. She wouldn't go so far as to say she trusted him, but she was certain that he wouldn't hurt her, and she didn't think he'd betray her.

'Okay,' she said. 'So, how will I know when it's time to visit you? And how will I get there?'

He gave her considering look. 'I will give you some notice and have someone come for you. I have many homes in different locations, so you might even find it enjoyable.'

The excitement inside her grew and she sat there, feeling the electricity of the sensation, half marvelling that she even knew what it was since she couldn't recall ever feeling excitement before.

Ares was now taking out his phone. He didn't look at her as he made a call, his rough voice filling the helicopter, speaking a language she didn't recognise.

Rose sat in the darkness, finally allowing the hope that she'd tried not to feel, that somehow hadn't died in all the years she'd been at the compound, to join the excitement that was already inside her. It felt like dawn breaking after a long, cold, dark night.

You owe it all to him.

She stole a glance at him, questions filling her head. Why did he want to marry? And why her? He was rich and powerful—all Vasiliev's guests were—and he must have many women to choose from, because he was certainly compelling despite his scars.

Did he really need someone like her? A woman who'd been a bought and sold servant all her life? A nobody who'd been cleaning his fireplace not a couple of hours ago?

It didn't make any sense.

Then again, maybe it didn't have to make sense. Because the main thing was that she was free. And she would have a whole year to herself, doing whatever she liked. Finding out where she came from…

She almost couldn't believe it was actually happening.

Some time passed, though she wasn't sure how long, and then the helicopter was descending. They landed in darkness and a few minutes later Rose found herself being ushered across a landing field and into a long, black car. The scarred man got into the car beside her, and she wanted to ask him where they were and what was happening, but the habit of keeping silent and staying guarded, and watching, was too deeply ingrained, so she said nothing as they drove into the night.

She'd find out soon enough, no doubt.

She must have dozed off because the next thing she knew, they were driving into a brightly lit city, though which one she had no idea. The car stopped outside a big, fancy-looking building, and she was ushered out of the car and up the steps and through the doors. The entrance-way was full of light, ornate chandeliers hanging from a lofty ceiling, and she stared at them, because they were beautiful and there hadn't been any in the compound.

There also seemed to be many people milling around all doing the scarred man's bidding.

He led the way to a bank of lifts and gestured her inside when the doors opened. She wasn't used to any kind of courtesy so the fact that he didn't push her inside or even touch her was almost disconcerting.

She got in, startling slightly as it began to ascend. But she didn't want him, or indeed anyone, to know just how disconcerting all of this was for her, so she kept her expression guarded.

When the lift arrived at the designated floor, she was taken down a long, silent hallway to a door, and when the door was opened and she was ushered inside, she realised it must be a hotel room.

She'd never been in a hotel room.

She had never been in a hotel at all.

Everything was beautifully appointed and there were big floor-to-ceiling windows that gave a nice view out over a city she didn't recognise. Not that she recognised any city, never having been in a city either.

There were several people already in the room, including a man in formal-looking robes who smiled at her.

The scarred man gave her a glance. 'Time to hold up your end of the bargain, Rose.'

She looked warily back. 'What do you mean?'

He nodded towards the man in formal robes. 'The priest will marry us.'

A small, electric shock arrowed through her. 'You mean…now?'

The scarred man shrugged. 'All the documentation you need will be easier to get if you are legally married to me.' His silver-green gaze was enigmatic. 'You do not have to be afraid. I will keep my word.'

He was trying to reassure her, she understood that. But she wasn't reassured, only annoyed. She wasn't some poor, helpless victim. And besides, she knew he kept his word, because he'd told her he'd rescue her and he had.

'I'm not afraid,' she said flatly. 'And I said I would marry you, so I will.'

He gave her another one of those long, speculative looks, then nodded in the direction of the priest.

Ignoring the strange clutch of trepidation, Rose moved over to where he stood, sensing the scarred man's huge, powerful presence at her side.

Her heartbeat was uncomfortably loud in her head as the priest began to say the words of the ceremony, but she didn't hesitate when it came to speaking her vows. And then she listened to his rough, scraping voice saying those same words.

'I, Ares Aristiades...'

Ares Aristiades. So, that was his name.

He didn't look at her as he said the words. She might as well not have been in the room. Not that she cared. This wasn't a marriage in any sense of the word, not yet. That would come later, and really, that was the least of her worries now.

She had greater concerns, such as what was going to happen next.

At the end of the ceremony, there were documents to sign, which she did.

'You don't have a second name?' the scarred man—Ares—asked, the first words he'd said personally to her since the ceremony.

'No,' she said. 'Perhaps I had one once, but I can't remember what it was. I'm just Rose.'

What he thought of that, she had no idea since he betrayed no reaction to the news whatsoever.

A few minutes later, a copy of the document was given to her.

'Here,' said Ares. 'Your marriage certificate.'

Rose looked down and saw her own name. *Rose Aristiades.*

It gave her a little jolt. For years and years, she'd had no last name. For years and years, she'd only been Rose. But now she wasn't. She had a last name now and a connection to someone.

She had a husband.

She looked up at him, but he'd already turned away, heading towards the door. He paused in the doorway and glanced back at her, enigmatic as a sphinx. 'I will see you in three months, Rose.'

Then he was gone.

CHAPTER THREE

Summer

ARES STOOD IN the middle of the villa's living area, looking through the big windows that faced the pool area, the deep, vivid green of the sea beyond it.

The pool was white stone and organically shaped with lots of flowing curves, and an infinity edge facing the ocean. Sun loungers in dark teak with white linen cushions stood around the pool, shaded by large white sun umbrellas. The garden surrounding the pool was lush and tropical, the scent of hibiscus and salt hanging heavy in the humid air flowing through the open windows of the villa.

A woman lay on one of the loungers. She was on her front, her head pillowed on her folded arms, the fading blue dye in her hair no match for the deep honey gold shining through it. The red bikini she wore fitted her as beautifully as he thought it would, lush curves spilling out of it, the sun highlighting a wealth of smooth, golden skin.

A sarong had been draped across the end of the lounger and on the low wooden table next to it stood a tall glass of orange juice and a book.

She'd been here in his villa, on a private island just near Koh Samui in Thailand, for a week already, which left him with only one more week of her presence. A pity, but he hadn't been able to get away sooner.

He'd wondered if she'd keep her promise to him when the time had arrived for their first two weeks. He'd thought the lure of travel might be enough, especially given the gleam he'd seen in her big golden eyes that night in the helicopter when he'd mentioned his different homes. And indeed, that seemed to be the case since here she was.

His wife. The little maid. Rose.

You should not have agreed to marry her.

No, perhaps he shouldn't have. Perhaps the urge that had taken him that night hadn't been one he should have listened to. He'd rescued her, as he'd promised, and he'd have given her all the help she'd needed to build a life for herself. He didn't require payment and he'd made certain that she knew that.

Except she'd insisted. She owed him, she'd

said, a fierce light gleaming in her pretty eyes. He'd bought her and so she owed him.

And no amount of telling her otherwise had made any difference, so when she'd asked him what he wanted, he'd told her. And when she'd said she'd be his wife in order to pay him back, he'd said he'd wanted children, thinking that then she'd surely give up insisting on this payment nonsense.

But she hadn't.

She clearly had *not* understood what she'd offered.

So perhaps that was why, in the end, he'd agreed. So he could show her.

Nothing at all to do with not being able to think about anything else but her in your bed.

He watched through the windows as Rose shifted on the sun lounger, burying her head deeper in her folded arms.

Yes, he'd admit to thinking that. Not that he'd touch her, or at least not until she decided to stay married to him—*if* she decided to stay married to him.

But in the meantime, he could deliver her a little lesson in what it meant to wildly promise things you didn't understand to people you shouldn't promise them to. And maybe he'd enjoy her company too. Naya wouldn't begrudge him that, surely?

Not that he'd had time to think too deeply about it in the past three months since their marriage.

He'd been very busy, involved in some new tech development and then a contract negotiation with one of the smaller Baltic states.

But Rose was always at the back of his mind. A puzzle he kept turning over and over, unable to put it down.

He was never interested in people. He was a tactician involved in the business of protecting them, but only as an abstract concept. Yet he couldn't deny that since he'd left her standing in that hotel room in Istanbul, having newly married her, he hadn't been able to stop thinking of her.

He wasn't sure why.

Perhaps it was how she had been the only woman to excite his lust in over a decade. Or perhaps it was how mysterious she was, how no one knew where she'd come from or even her real name. Or maybe it was more to do with how she hadn't been afraid of him, even from the first moment they'd met. Even in that helicopter, full of wariness and suspicion, trepidation and apprehension, she'd met his gaze determinedly as she'd put her offer of marriage to him.

It was clear then that she had no idea what it meant to be your wife, and yet still you accepted.

Out beside the pool, Rose shifted yet again, the sunlight gleaming on her skin.

No, she didn't know. That's why he'd decided to give her a year of freedom for herself, while at the same time, she would spend two weeks every season to get to know him. And if at the end of a year, she did not want to remain married, he would annul the marriage.

Naya wouldn't object to that.

He pulled his phone out of his pocket and glanced at the screen, once more scrolling through the emails one of his assistants had sent him, providing him with all the info he needed about what his wife had been doing for the past three months.

She'd been living in Paris, in an apartment she'd found herself rather than the one he'd organised for her. She'd also found herself a job waiting tables at a local cafe, which she hadn't needed to do since he'd provided enough money for her, and yet she'd insisted on anyway.

Strange when she was the one who'd asked for his help. She was apparently very set on doing things her own way according to the staff member he'd assigned to help her, and did not like to be told what to do. That, he could understand. She'd been a prisoner for so long, and some people would have been beaten down by it.

Not Rose.

She'd adapted very quickly to life outside the compound, learning French and English in rapid succession, as well as opening her own bank account. Apart from some initial set-up money, she hadn't touched any of the funds he'd provided, preferring to live frugally off her own wages at the cafe.

Again, odd when she'd been the one to request the money.

It made him curious. It made him want to know more.

He'd made some initial enquiries to track down where she came from, but so far hadn't had any luck. He'd assumed she was Russian, but maybe she wasn't. Maybe she'd come from somewhere else.

He put his phone away and gazed at her through the windows, the breeze ruffling her hair that tumbled over her shoulders. He had no idea why she'd dyed it blue, but the afternoon sunlight caught gleams of brightness in among the dark blue strands, like a seam of gold at the bottom of the ocean.

Pretty.

Yes. And so was she.

His plan for this next week was simply to get her used to his presence, nothing more, no matter what his body wanted. Sex would happen when and if she decided she wanted to stay married to him, and not before.

He had once been an exemplary legionnaire, a master of himself physically, and impatience had never been one of his weaknesses. Still, it had been a long time since he'd been with a woman, and he couldn't deny a certain...hunger.

A strange thrill wound through him, and he realised with a start that it was anticipation. He'd been looking forward to this. When had that last happened? He couldn't remember.

Yes, you do. Going home after a day on the mountains and seeing Naya.

But that had been years ago, and Naya was long dead. He'd had a terrible lesson in the dangers of allowing his emotions to blind him, and he'd learned it. Love was the weakness. Love had exacerbated the flaws in his pride and his arrogance, making him think that as a descendent of Hercules, nothing could touch him. But he'd been wrong.

He was just a man and not a particularly good one at that.

Moving over to the big glass doors that had been pushed back to allow the breeze to flow into the house, Ares stepped out into the pool area. He walked silently over to the sun lounger where she lay and stopped beside it, glancing down at her.

She didn't stir.

The last time he'd seen her, she'd been in that black dress with her hair in a bun. Now, though, she wore only the bikini, and the curves that had only been hinted at by her dress were on full display. And yes, they were as spectacular as he'd thought they would be. Full, rounded breasts and generous hips and thighs, elegant back, small waist, shapely rear...

Her golden skin gleamed and lust kicked hard inside him. He caught his breath, conscious that he hadn't felt so intensely about anything for years, let alone a woman. He even had the oddest need to run a finger lightly down her spine, see how warm her skin felt, how silky and smooth. Touch her purely for the sensuality of it.

You felt this way about Naya, remember?

Oh, he remembered. He'd seen her that night in a crowded bar in Athens, getting hassled by some lowlife. Dark eyes, dark hair, a glowingly beautiful face. She'd been gracious and polite, but the man bothering her was not and Ares had had to teach him a few lessons in courtesy. Afterwards, Ares had bought her a drink and been captivated instantly and so had she with him. Their physical attraction had been so powerful they'd ended up in her hotel room only an hour later...

He wasn't that young man, completely at the

mercy of his body's needs, not any more. The years in the Legion, concentrating on nothing but honing his physical skills and obeying orders, had been well spent. No passing fancy or rogue emotion escaped his control nowadays.

So, he ignored the heat that burned inside him. Ignored the urge to touch her. Physical desire was no match for his will. He'd already decided how this first week would go and it did not include any physical closeness.

For now, he'd let her know he was here, inform her they'd be having dinner together and then he'd retire to his office for the afternoon. That was all.

'Good afternoon, Rose,' he said, his voice a heavy rasp in the peaceful silence.

She jerked, her head lifting sharply, her eyes meeting his.

He remembered those eyes, large and golden. He remembered her heart-shaped face and her small, precise features. The feline tilt of her golden brows, the soft little rosebud of her mouth.

She was beautiful and he hadn't fully comprehended that until now.

Perhaps that was why the lust inside him kicked harder, deeper. Why his fingers curled unconsciously in the pockets of his trousers, clenching tight, as if to stop from reaching for her.

Nothing else would explain this ridiculous re-action to a woman he barely knew. One look at her beauty and a decade of celibacy that hadn't weighed on him at all now felt heavier than an entire planet.

Her eyes had widened, taking him in, shock rippling over her face. Then the shock disap-peared as quickly as it had come, her expression becoming as guarded and wary as he remem-bered.

Slowly, she sat up, treating him to a view of full, pretty breasts almost spilling over the cups of her red bikini, and much to his intense an-noyance, the more disobedient parts of himself began to harden.

Theos, what was happening? He wasn't fif-teen any more. The mere sight of a woman's breasts in a small bikini top should not make him hard. He'd decided nothing would be hap-pening between them and so nothing would, regardless of what his baser parts were urging.

Clearly noticing the direction of his gaze, she coloured and reached for the sarong, quickly wrapping the material around herself.

He made no comment. There was no point drawing attention to his own interest or her modesty. If she wanted to remain his wife after this year had passed, then they could have that discussion, but that time wasn't now.

'Good afternoon…uh…' she said, her soft, husky voice trailing off uncertainly. 'Mr Aristiades?' Her damp hair had fallen around her shoulders in thick waves, vivid gold glinting in among the strands of blue.

'My name is Ares,' he said, more tersely than he'd intended. 'I am your husband, remember?'

The pink in her cheeks deepened into red, a flash of temper glinting in her eyes. 'I hadn't forgotten. That's why I'm here. Which I have been, for an entire week.'

Intriguing. It seemed she was annoyed with him. He hadn't thought she'd care that he hadn't been here when she'd arrived. He'd even thought she'd enjoy having a week to herself. Yet was that not the case?

'I had business to attend to,' he said. 'As I'm sure my staff informed you.'

'They did, I just thought…' She stopped.

He lifted a brow. 'You thought what?'

'It doesn't matter.' She fussed with the material of her sarong, making a knot between her breasts. 'I'm here anyway. As you ordered.'

He was tempted to push her on whatever it was that didn't matter and why exactly she was so annoyed, but decided it could wait until dinner. Right now, he was here to inform her of his arrival, nothing more.

'Indeed, you are,' he murmured, his gaze

dropping to where her hands fussed with the knot of her sarong, drawing attention to the shadowed valley between her breasts. He could imagine undoing that knot and tugging aside the cup of her bikini, letting one full breast spill into his palm…

No. *Theos*, this had to stop.

Ares had to consciously drag his gaze back to her face. Yet again, she must have noticed him looking, because another blush turned her cheeks a deep rose and her hands had dropped away from the knot.

Irritation with himself and his recalcitrant body coiled like a snake in his gut, though a distant part of him found it interesting that she was blushing instead of showing any fear. He'd thought it likely that she'd been manhandled back in the compound because she was beautiful and no doubt there had been men who'd viewed her as something they could take. The chances of her being untouched were remote and so he was expecting fear not embarrassment.

Yet he didn't think it was fear that made her blush.

'You will have to get used to me looking at you, little maid,' he said, since there was no point denying he hadn't been, and since if he was going to teach her exactly what she'd got herself into, he might as well start right now. 'That is what a husband does with a wife. He also does more than look. Especially if he wants children.' He watched her face for fear as he said it, or even trepidation. But there was none.

Instead, that small spark of temper glittered brighter in her eyes.

Three months earlier he'd noticed that spark, the flicker of a warrior spirit, and it seemed that the past three months of freedom had only fanned the flames.

Good. He liked that. It was better than the guardedness she'd displayed earlier and definitely better than fear.

You never wanted a doormat for a wife.

No. No, he did not.

'Fine, then let's get on with trying for them now,' she said tartly. 'Might as well get the first attempt over and done with.'

For a second, he almost laughed and then realised she wasn't joking. She truly did not understand, did she?

'Little maid,' he said with some patience. 'That is not what we agreed on. I told you that claiming my rights as a husband would only happen if and when you decide to stay married to me. And only after a year has passed.' He gave her a direct look. 'And if you decide to stay, there will be no "getting it over and done with" about any attempt at children. Do you understand me?'

She scowled. 'It's just sex. What do you care?'

Ares opened his mouth. Closed it again. Then pondered an appropriate response. She didn't seem to be scared at the thought of sleeping with him. She could be pretending, of course, but he didn't think she was. Had she managed to escape assault while in the compound? Or maybe she hadn't. Maybe she'd become inured to it.

At that thought, the sullen anger he'd experienced in Ivan's study that night flickered to life inside once again. At what might have happened to Rose and how helpless she would have been to stop it. Again, he did not appreciate the feeling.

Over the past three months he'd been steadily gathering information on Ivan and his business. He was still pondering the best course of action, but was erring on the side of armed men storming Ivan's house and legalities be damned.

It was no less than what the man deserved.

'That is something we can discuss later tonight,' he said at last, deciding this was not the time to talk about it. 'Over dinner.'

'Dinner?' She didn't sound any less irritated by this. 'That's what you came here for? Dinner?'

'I am here so we can get to know one another,' he said mildly. 'So, you have some idea about what being a wife means. And dinner is part of that. In fact, I have dinner planned every night—'

'No,' Rose interrupted flatly.

Ares blinked, completely nonplussed. 'No? What do you mean no?'

'You didn't marry me to get to know me.' She was looking distinctly angry now. 'You married me because you wanted children. That's what you said. So, let's have sex and then I can leave, because I have other, more important things to do than hang around waiting for you.'

Rose stared angrily at her husband, totally forgetting that she'd decided to take a wary and watchful approach to him, and not to let her temper get the better of her.

But she'd been waiting a week for him, winding herself up with imagining what would happen when he arrived, and getting herself into quite a state. She was angry she hadn't been told exactly what these first two weeks would entail—he'd said it would be so they could get to know one another, but what did that mean?—and then even more angry to find that when she'd arrived, he wasn't here. That he'd been delayed a whole week, leaving her to stew about what would happen when he finally arrived.

She knew she should stay in control of her

emotions, that there was a reason she should keep them locked away, but three months of freedom had allowed her more emotional expression than she'd ever had in her life, and she liked it.

Oh, she'd tried to enjoy herself too—she'd never been to Thailand and his villa on a secluded island was more luxury than she'd ever seen—but anger felt good, it felt powerful, and so she indulged it.

That night in the helicopter, he'd told her she owed him nothing, yet she knew she'd never truly be free unless she got rid of all ties, all obligations, and so she'd insisted he marry her. He'd agreed. It had seemed like an excellent plan at the time, but now she'd had time to process what had happened and, quite frankly, she was having second thoughts.

It had seemed so clear that night. He'd given her what she wanted and so she'd give him what he wanted. That was how the world had worked in the compound, and now that she was out, it seemed that was how it worked everywhere else too. Things were bought and sold, sometimes for money, sometimes for favours, sometimes for services, but nothing came for free.

The first month she'd decided that out of necessity she'd use some of the funds her powerful husband had set aside for her, but in the future, it was better not to rely on him. So, she'd found a job and an apartment, and even though she didn't earn much, she made sure she lived within her means and had some left over for savings.

She was enjoying being self-sufficient and wasn't in any hurry to live with him, be a wife to him like she'd seen in the movies or TV. Where wives seemed to worry over the well-being of their husbands, have difficulties with children, argue about money and get annoyed about sex.

That didn't look like freedom to her.

However, she *had* promised she'd come to him for two weeks of every season and she would. Except he hadn't been clear what 'getting to know each other' actually meant. She'd assumed it was just another way of saying he expected sex. That was usually what men wanted, no matter what they said.

She was fine with sex. She'd prepared herself for it.

Yet now, here he was, telling her that no, he didn't expect that and in fact what he wanted was dinner. *Dinner.*

It didn't help that he'd startled her awake, his rasping voice somehow insinuating itself in a dream she was having about lying naked on the sun lounger with someone stroking her bare back very lightly, making her shiver and not with fear.

She'd been enjoying it, until he'd said her name and she'd woken up with a start to find him standing next to her, staring down at her.

That silver-green gaze of his was just as haunting as it had been three months earlier, those deep scars just as horrifying. The proud, stark planes and angles of his face just as mesmerising.

He wore a crisp white business shirt, and dark blue suit trousers, and standing there with his hands in his pockets, his broad, powerful figure looming over her, the force of his presence had been like a hammer blow.

He'd looked at her in the way a man looks at a woman he wants, and she knew that because men had looked at her that way before. She'd always hated it. It made her frightened and then angry, because if they'd wanted to do anything about it, she couldn't stop them.

But now, even though she could stop him, it was worse. Because when he looked at her, she didn't feel frightened. She felt...prickly. Shivery. As if she liked him looking at her, which couldn't be right.

She didn't like it. She didn't. And she *did* have more important things to do. Such as continuing the search for who she was. For anything that could give her a clue about her real identity. She hadn't found anything yet, but that didn't mean there wasn't anything to find. She hadn't given up wanting to escape the compound and she had, and she wouldn't give this up either.

Ares raised one black brow again, infuriatingly calm. 'What important things do you have to do, little maid?'

'Don't call me that,' she snapped. 'I'm not a maid any more.'

His other brow rose. 'True. But Rose isn't your name either, is it?'

She wasn't surprised he knew about her origins—or rather, her lack of them. She'd done her research on him as soon as she could. Ares Aristiades, owner of Hercules Security, a worldwide security company that provided military services to governments the world over. There wasn't much about him on the internet, not that she was surprised about that either. He was a man who stayed out of the spotlight, which she could understand given his business and the secrecy that it no doubt entailed.

What other information she'd managed to find was sparse. He'd been born to a hardscrabble life in the mountains of Greece as a shepherd before going into the French Foreign Legion and carving a military career for himself that many would be proud of. Then he'd built himself a billion-dollar company by being one of the best military tacticians on the planet.

A mysterious man with a questionable company and who knew Vasiliev.

She didn't like what that said about him, despite the fact that he'd rescued her. She didn't want to be a wife to a man who condoned the buying and selling of people like herself, or associated with those who did the buying and selling.

No, she didn't like that, and she didn't like him.

Now, she glared angrily at him. 'My name could be Rose. You don't know.'

'It's unlikely.'

'It doesn't matter how unlikely it is, it still could be.' She sniffed. 'Anyway, that doesn't matter. I have decided my name is Rose so that's what it is.'

He regarded her for a long moment, his expression inscrutable. 'You are not the same woman you were three months ago, are you?'

'What? A biddable servant you can do anything with? An object that you can ignore? No, I am not.' She glanced up at him from beneath her lashes, a daring thought occurring to her. If she played with the knot of her sarong, what would he do? Would it irritate him? Would it knock that annoyingly expressionless expression from his face? He'd left her stewing for a whole week and part of her wanted to make him stew too.

Some of the other cleaning women in the compound had whispered about using their sexuality to make men do what they wanted, but Rose had never seen the point of it. If it wasn't going to get her out of captivity, then why bother?

But perhaps she could understand it now. Like anger, there was a certain...power to it. Men were easy to manipulate, or so some of the others had said.

Maybe she could test her own power, see what it did to him. Experiment a little.

She lifted her hand and fussed with the knot, watching him slyly as she did so.

One corner of his twisted mouth turned up, though the rest of his face remained impassive. Was his lack of expression due to all that scar tissue perhaps?

'I am not going to do what you want, Rose,' he said. 'No matter how many times you play with that knot.'

Damn. Either he wasn't open to manipulation, or he didn't want her as much as she'd thought.

She let her hand drop and pulled a face. 'What's the point of getting to know one another? When all you want from a wife is children?'

He gave her a steady look. 'Are you a virgin, Rose?'

After years of staying quiet and still and keeping her secrets, her instinct was not to tell him. But she wasn't in the compound now, and anyway, there wasn't much point in hiding it. 'Yes,' she said, lifting her chin in challenge.

His eyes widened a fraction. 'No one touched you? No one...hurt you?'

The question stung. That she'd managed to avoid what many of the others hadn't made her uncomfortable, not to mention angry. 'Vasiliev's daughter, Athena, was my friend. She...protected me.' She gave him a severe look. 'Not that it didn't stop men from trying to take what wasn't theirs.'

He remained inscrutable. 'I see.'

'It doesn't bother you?' she asked suddenly, wanting to know. 'That you bought me? That I was sold to you? Were you okay with it? Or perhaps you take part in it yourself?'

Again, his expression gave nothing away. 'No,' he said flatly. 'I do not. And no, I was not okay with it.'

'Really? Because you look okay with it.'

'If you hadn't noticed, I do not have a lot of

movement in my face.' His voice was terse. 'It does not mean I was okay with it, not in any way.'

That wasn't fair. You thought it might be scar tissue, so why push?

A small thread of guilt wound through her, but she ignored it. Why shouldn't she push? He hadn't told her anything about himself and she needed to know.

'So why were you there? In Vasiliev's compound?'

Finally, an emotion flickered across his ruined face, but she couldn't tell what it was. 'Vasiliev was my father-in-law, once upon a time. I visit him every year.'

Rose blinked, taken off-guard. His father-in-law? She'd made up all kinds of reasons for why Ares would be at the compound. Good reasons, she realised with a start, because she hadn't wanted him to be there for bad reasons. She hadn't wanted him to be like all the others who visited Vasiliev.

That means he was married.

Rose blinked again. 'You're married? I mean, to someone else?'

Ares gave her an enigmatic glance. 'Once. A long time ago.'

'But what happened—'

'We'll talk tonight,' he interrupted, his tone

casual yet firm. 'I'll have one of the staff come and get you when dinner is served.'

Then before she could say another word, he turned and stalked back into the villa, leaving her staring after him.

She didn't know what to make of that. She didn't know what to make of him, full stop.

She'd never thought that a man so hard and impassive, so seemingly wrought of iron, would do something so mundane as visit his ex-father-in-law.

It was…interesting, she couldn't deny it. She was married to this man, after all, and while technically she didn't have to stay married to him, she had given her word she'd spend two weeks of every season with him. And she was here now.

Perhaps it wouldn't be such a bad idea to get to know him, as he'd said.

Anyway, that was the least of her worries. She'd been thinking more and more about Athena, still trapped in that place. Kept in luxury and pampered, it was true, but still a prisoner.

Vasiliev needed taking down.

You can help her.

Rose bit her lip, staring sightlessly at the villa. Well, she wanted to, but how? She had no money and no power. And she didn't know anyone who… Wait a second…

Ares.

Yes, he could help. He had the money and the power. He had the means, and she was his wife. She could ask him, couldn't she? He might not agree—it was difficult to tell what he thought about anything—but... Maybe she wasn't without something to bargain with.

She touched the knot of her sarong, remembering how his gaze had dropped there when she'd fussed around tying it. There had been heat in his gaze and perhaps she could use that. He'd said he wasn't going to do anything no matter how she played with that knot, but was he really as controlled as he made out? He'd declined the first time she'd offered herself, up in that room in the compound, and he'd just refused her now, which meant a straight-up offer of sex didn't move him.

She would have to do something more.

Still thinking, Rose slipped off the sun lounger and walked towards the big glass doors of the villa, stepping inside.

The past week she'd spent here on her own had been very pleasant. She'd done nothing but swim and lie around the pool reading books she'd found in the small library near her own room. In fact, she hadn't been able to get enough of books. She'd been given a bare minimum of an education in Vasiliev's compound, enough to read and write and some basic sums, so in the past three months she'd gorged herself on information.

She loved reading. There was something about escaping into another world and joining the characters of whatever book she was in the middle of, experiencing their journey with them that was very exciting. And it wasn't just fiction she devoured, but nonfiction too, all kinds from science to technology, history to philosophy, and everything in between.

Most of the books in the library were in English, but there were a few in a strange-looking language that she'd discovered was Greek. The script looked familiar to her, which was even stranger, though she couldn't imagine why.

She moved down the wide, breezy hallway, the dark wood of the floor gleaming as she made her way to her bedroom. It was situated in one wing of the villa that overlooked sharp cliffs, a green, translucent sea swirling around the base. The big windows were open to let in the humid air, while slatted screens drawn across them prevented any rogue insects.

A big four-poster bed piled high with white pillows was pushed up against one wall, the frothy mosquito net canopy pulled back. The bed had been made by the villa's staff and she'd run a professional eye over it before she could stop herself. Initially she'd been suspicious of the staff here and had asked the housekeeper many questions about whether they were actually staff who'd been hired and who were paid regularly, since her experience of staff in rich people's houses was that 'staff' was a very loose term. But the housekeeper had patiently explained that yes, the people who worked here were indeed staff and that Mr Aristiades paid them well.

She'd been encouraged by that, but not enough to trust him, of course.

Wandering over to the big dresser carved in a gleaming, dark wood, Rose pulled open a couple of drawers, thinking. When she'd arrived, she'd found the wardrobe and the dresser full of clothes and all in her size. Ares had obviously prepared for her even though she'd brought her own meagre supply of clothing.

Everything was beautifully made, in gorgeous fabrics, and obviously very expensive, and secretly she loved that he'd provided a few extra items. She'd had to check with the housekeeper—the poor woman had the patience of a saint—about why there were clothes in the drawers and the housekeeper had been very clear that they were for her. So, she'd spent at least a couple of hours going through all the beautiful things and admiring them. She'd never had anything so beautiful, and she found herself being slightly less suspicious of him than she'd been before. But only slightly. She still needed to be cautious.

Now, she rifled through a drawer and pulled out a gorgeous silk sarong in vivid golds and blues. There were gowns hanging in the wardrobe, but she didn't want to wear a gown for dinner tonight. She didn't want to look as if she was trying too hard. Yet she also wanted to look beautiful, because if she was going to bargain with him, she needed something to offer. Herself.

Again.

Yes, again. She just had to find out what would move him. What would…seduce him.

She held the sarong up and examined it critically. It was a little see-through, but not too much. At least, she hoped it wasn't too much because perhaps it was temptation he needed. A glimpse of what he could have, rather than everything immediately.

Carrying the sarong over to the bed, she laid it down on the white quilt.

Was she really going to do this? She'd spent years avoiding men's gazes, afraid of their touch, yet now she was considering actively courting one man's attention.

A man she didn't know and didn't trust. A

man who'd bought her and married her, yet freed her.

She didn't understand that. When a man wanted something, he took it; that had been her experience and so while she understood him buying her and agreeing to marry her, she still didn't understand why he'd then let her go. Or why he wanted to 'get to know her.' Or 'dinner.' In the helicopter that night, he'd mentioned teaching her what it meant to be a wife, which had been kind of patronising of him, but was all of this part of the lesson?

Whatever, she wasn't here to understand him. She was here because she'd agreed to come, and her word was important to her. And because she'd decided that, since she was here she might as well use him the way he was using her.

She touched the silk on the bed, the material light and insubstantial against her fingertips.

He'd said she was a different woman than she'd been three months ago, and yes, she was. She didn't know what kind of woman she truly was, not when she'd grown up in that place and not when that had moulded her in a certain way, but she wanted to find out. Part of her freedom was the freedom to choose who she wanted to be and she could be anyone, couldn't she?

But how can you ever truly know who you are, when you don't even know who you were?

That would come. She'd find out. She would.

In the meantime, she would choose simply not being a victim. Or a servant or a poor trafficked girl.

She would choose to be powerful. Strong and in control. A seductress.

Let him deal with that.

CHAPTER FOUR

ARES SAT AT the table reading an email on his laptop. Night had fallen abruptly, as it did in the tropics, the air heavy with humidity and the scent of flowers. The darkness was broken by the discreet lighting of the outside terrace, the thick trees and shrubs highlighted with various spotlights.

Candles in glass hurricane lamps had been placed on the table, along with a full silver service in preparation for dinner. Crystal wine glasses and white porcelain, snowy napkins and a gleaming silver ice bucket for the champagne.

His staff had outdone themselves and he was pleased.

Except that Rose was late.

It annoyed him, though he tried not to let it. His days in the Legion had taught him to be adaptable and not everyone was as punctual as he was. Though these days, everyone ran to his

command, and he was not used to people dis-
obeying his orders.

He did not look at his watch. She was making him wait, he was sure of it.

Anticipation gathered inside him, though he
tried to ignore that too. The anticipation of an
unexpected challenge, because she was unexpected.

He hadn't expected that little scene by the
pool, for example, her being cross with him and
offering to get the sex 'over and done with' as
if it didn't matter. She'd been all prickly, not
bothering to hide her annoyance with him at
being made to wait a whole week for him to
arrive, and he was male enough to find it sat-
isfying that she was impatient. That she'd been
thinking of him.

*You fool. Why should you care who she's
thinking of?*

He didn't. But he could enjoy a woman thinking of him, couldn't he? It had been years, after
all. He'd also rather enjoyed her trying to tempt
him by toying with the knot of her sarong. A
long time since he'd played that game with a
woman too, and he couldn't deny a certain pleasure in playing it with Rose.

Except he hadn't enjoyed her mentioning
Ivan. Or how he'd let slip Ivan's relationship
to him. He couldn't think why he had. Maybe

it had been her thinking he was a human trafficker, or perhaps condoned it, and he'd felt... angry. Yet again.

He hadn't wanted her thinking that of him, though why her opinion mattered he couldn't fathom.

She was his wife, it was true, but only in a legal sense. Their marriage wasn't based on any kind of emotion.

No, your marriage is based on a debt she feels she owes you.

He frowned down at his laptop, turning that thought over in his head.

That was an issue. She'd never be free, she'd told him that night in the helicopter, not until she'd paid him back, and while he understood her reasoning, he didn't like it. What must it have been like, growing up in Ivan's compound? Imprisoned, knowing that she was property...

The anger that had ignited three months earlier burned hotter now, smouldering like an ember in his chest, and he rubbed at it, trying to ignore it.

It was terrible what had happened to Rose, but he could not afford to personalise it. He'd learned many things in the years since his wife had been gone, and not allowing his emotions to get the better of his intellect was one of those things.

For example, if he'd known back then that Stavros and his gang of petty thugs would retaliate so violently, he wouldn't have allowed his pride to get in the way and would have paid the protection money they'd demanded. But he hadn't. He hadn't wanted Naya to think him a coward. Aristiades was a proud name, and strong, and he'd refused to bow to weaker men.

Yet those weaker men had torched his house, and Naya had been killed. Her life the price of his pride.

He should never have allowed himself such arrogance. He should have thought things through. He should have thought, full stop.

A soft footfall came from the direction of the double doors that led from the dining room and out onto the terrace.

Ares dragged his attention from his laptop screen.

Rose stood in the doorway. Her hair was loose over her shoulders, the candlelight picking up strands of brilliant honey gold in amongst the blue, and she wore a silk sarong in blue and gold wrapped around her lush figure as a dress, the ends twisted and tied at her nape to create a halter neck. On her feet she wore flat golden sandals, golden ties crisscrossing up her calves.

The silk billowed gently around her in the breeze, and he realised, with a start, that the silk was just a little transparent, giving him tantalising, shadowy glimpses of her curves. Making it very clear that she wore nothing underneath it.

Desire leapt inside him, and he had to concentrate very hard on staying exactly where he was and not moving an inch simply to stay in control.

She came slowly down the steps that led from the doorway to the terrace, the silk swirling around her legs, the fabric parting to reveal a hint of pale golden thigh.

She was beautiful, utterly beautiful. And it was clear that she knew it and that she was using it as some kind of power play, because as she came over to the table, the look she gave him from beneath those thick golden lashes was speculative. Assessing.

His little maid had come to the fight armed and was now sizing up her opponent.

Interesting. Very interesting.

He didn't know which particular battle she wanted to engage him in, or what she thought she was fighting for, but he'd oblige her. He might even allow her a victory if the mood took him, because she couldn't win, not if he didn't let her.

Ignoring the desire that gripped him, Ares rose to his feet. He came around the table, pulled out her chair and held out a hand, inviting her to sit.

She gave a little frown, as if she hadn't been expecting that, but made no comment, sitting down gracefully. She smelled sweet, like lilies, clearly having availed herself of one of the many different bath oils stocked in her bathroom.

Ares pushed her chair in, anticipation gathering in his gut at the coming fight, especially with such a worthy opponent.

It was only supposed to be dinner, remember?

Of course. And it would only be dinner no matter how many games she wanted to play.

Stepping back from her chair, he went over to where the champagne was cooling in the ice bucket and lifted it. 'A drink to celebrate?' he asked casually.

A flicker of irritation crossed her face, as if that wasn't what she hoped he'd say, and then was gone. Carefully and with some ceremony, she adjusted the folds of her sarong. 'Celebrate what?'

Ares couldn't help himself. He was amused at her annoyance and further amused by her attempts to hide it. 'Our marriage,' he said, opening the champagne and popping the cork. 'Though you aren't here for a celebration, are you? You're here for a fight.'

More emotions chased themselves over her

face, though they were gone too fast for him to get a good glimpse of what they were. She was much more expressive than she had been three months earlier, as he'd already noted. Had that guardedness been a legacy of growing up in Ivan's compound? Had she had to monitor herself all the time, to make sure she gave nothing away?

What must it have been like for her? Constantly under threat, constantly waiting for an attack. She was a prisoner of war, living with the enemy, nothing but property...

The smouldering anger tugged at the leash he'd put on it, but he dismissed it. Curiosity and desire he'd allow, but nothing more than that.

'A fight?' she echoed as he poured some champagne into her glass. 'What makes you say that?'

'The fact that you are wearing a transparent sarong with nothing on underneath it.' He poured champagne for himself, dumped the bottle back in the ice bucket and sat down. Then he lifted his glass. 'To my beautiful wife.'

Rose did not lift her glass. She stared at him, her chin jutting stubbornly. 'I don't want to fight you.'

Ares shrugged and took a sip of his champagne. 'You want something, though.'

Her pretty mouth compressed with annoyance. Clearly, he was not supposed to have spotted that. 'Well,' she said. 'Since you didn't seem to want what I offered at the pool, I thought I'd give you a preview of…what you said no to.'

He sat back in his chair as another unfamiliar, disquieting emotion flexed inside him. It felt like guilt, though he couldn't think about what. Not that he'd refused her, that had been the right thing to do, and he didn't need to think of Naya to know that. More because of what she'd thought she had to do in order to engage his attention, bargaining for something with her body…

Was that the way it had worked at Vasiliev's? And did she really think he was the kind of man who indulged in such bargains? He'd refused her twice already and still she tried to give herself to him, so it was clear she did.

He didn't like it.

'You want something, Rose.' Might as well be direct about it. 'So why don't you tell me what it is?'

She bit her lip a moment, frowning at him, as if she was weighing something up. Then she said flatly, 'I want your help freeing my friend Athena in Vasiliev's compound.'

He frowned. 'What do you mean Athena? She's Ivan's daughter.'

Rose shook her head. 'She's not. She was

bought at the same time I was. I came to the compound with her.'

Ares had to admit to a certain shock.

He hadn't known that about Athena. His mother-in-law had been devastated after Naya's death, and after Ares had been discharged from the hospital and before he'd gone into the Legion, he'd visited both her and Ivan. But she'd taken one look at him and had fled the room. The burns, the reminder of what happened to her daughter, had been too much for her.

She never came when he visited Ivan, and when he'd heard that they'd adopted a child, he hadn't enquired further. He had his own grief to deal with.

Except it appeared she'd hadn't been adopted, after all. Athena was a trafficked child and Ivan must have bought her for his wife, that was the only explanation.

You should have known this. You should have known exactly what Ivan was doing, but you wanted to give him the benefit of the doubt. For Naya's sake.

Ares looked down at the champagne glass he held in his hand, the ember in his chest that despite his best efforts to ignore it hadn't gone out, a constant burning pain.

It was clear he had to do something about this. Ivan had always been…shady in his business dealings, but those first few years, he'd been consumed with grief as well as recovering from his injuries, and he hadn't noticed anything untoward at the compound. Then he'd gone into the Legion and when he'd come out again he'd been shaped into something much harder, all his weaknesses—his pride and all the other, useless emotions that went along with it—shorn away.

Naya's memory was his conscience, his guide as to what was right, and she had loved her father, despite his numerous flaws. So, Ares had ignored his doubts about Ivan, continuing with his visits, doing his duty to Naya.

Perhaps you didn't do anything because you didn't want to. Because you prefer not caring. Because it keeps you safe.

Ares shoved that particular thought away.

'Ivan will not let Athena go,' he said after a moment, still staring into his champagne. 'Not if his wife has any say about it.'

'That doesn't mean I can't try,' Rose insisted. 'She helped me. She protected me. I can't leave her there.'

Ares looked up to find Rose's direct golden gaze staring straight into his. And she didn't look away. There was a steely determination in it, as if nothing and no one would dissuade her from her path, let alone him.

She cares about her friend.

He found that unsettling, even as the fierce look on her face appealed to the warrior in him, sending a flicker of intense heat straight to his groin. It made him want to match her, test her, conquer her. She was even more attractive to him now, all fire and spirit, and iron at her heart.

He didn't look away either. 'So, what are you asking me, Rose?'

'Isn't it obvious? I want you to get Athena out.'

'And I assume you will want to pay me for my assistance?'

'Of course.' She held out her arms. 'If you help me, you can have me. Whenever and however you want.'

Ares's silver-green gaze betrayed nothing. He lounged opposite her at the table, long, powerful legs stretched out, his champagne glass held casually in one hand. Unlike her, he hadn't changed for dinner, still wearing that pristine white shirt and the suit trousers that emphasised his muscular thighs.

The candlelight cast flickering shadows across his ruined face, turning his scars into a horrifying kind of architecture. Part beauty, part nightmare, and unsettling.

This is a stupid idea. He's already said no to you twice. What makes you think he'll agree now?

Well, she didn't know if he'd agree. But she hoped. And this was different. She wasn't a prisoner now and after three months in the outside world she knew more than she had. She wasn't a powerless victim with nothing but her body to bargain with.

And apart from anything else, he wanted her.

Nervous tension coiled inside her. She hadn't expected to put forward her offer so early on in the evening, but not only was he not stupid, he was also very direct. He'd guessed straight away that she'd wanted something from him. Which was fine. She liked his directness, but it didn't leave her with much negotiation room.

'But I've already refused your generous offer,' he pointed out. Irritatingly. 'Twice. What makes you think I'll accept it now?'

Rose grabbed her champagne glass and took a sip. It was very dry and very cold, and she liked it. 'Because you want me.' She glared at him over the rim of her glass. 'I can see it in your eyes.'

His expression was enigmatic, his gaze opaque. 'But you do not want me, Rose. That is the issue.'

Unexpectedly a little thrill pulsed through her. He hadn't denied it. He *did* want her. But as for her not wanting him, well, that was a lie. Sex sounded uncomfortable, yet she wouldn't mind if she had to do it with him. He wouldn't hurt her, she didn't think.

'I do want you,' she insisted. 'I said I'd give you children, didn't I?'

'Sex is not a transaction, little maid. Or at least, it shouldn't be. That is why I said you could have a year to make up your mind about whether you wanted to stay married to me. You should choose it because you want it.'

She frowned, not liking the overly patient tone in his voice. She was very inexperienced, it was true, but she wasn't a child. 'But I did want it. I was the one who suggested the whole marriage thing in the first place, remember?'

His head tilted slightly, his eyes glittering in the candlelight. 'Yes. To pay off a debt I told you that you did not have to pay.'

'I might not *have* to pay it but it's a debt all the same,' she insisted. 'And anyway, you agreed. It wasn't as if I held a gun to your head and demanded that you marry me or else.'

'True,' he said. 'You did not.' And oddly another one of those smiles turned his mouth, as if he was enjoying her responses, making something in her stomach flutter like a bird. It was genuine amusement, she thought, and it lightened his face. He would never be an easy man to be around, his presence was too intense, too overwhelming for that, but it lessened the claustrophobic weight of it. Made her almost want to smile with him.

'What's so funny?' she asked, irritated with how hot her cheeks suddenly felt.

'You are a surprising woman, Rose.' He surveyed her from underneath ridiculously thick, silky black lashes. 'I was not expecting that.'

Warmth shifted inside her, as if part of her was very pleased to be thought of as surprising by him. Again, unsettling. In fact, he was unsettling all round.

She shifted in her chair. 'What were you expecting then? A doormat?'

'No. I like a woman who speaks her own mind and isn't afraid to match wills with me.'

Again, there was that flutter deep inside her, an excited little thrill. Part of her liked that very much indeed. Liked that a man as iron hard as he was thought she was strong enough to match wills with. And that he wanted her to speak her mind.

He might call you little maid, but he's never treated you like one.

That was very true. Every time she'd been on cleaning duty in his room while he was Vasiliev's guest, he'd never told her what to do the way some did. He'd never treated her like a piece of furniture. He'd been...aware of her.

And it had never made her feel afraid.

You liked it. He interested you.

Rose shifted in her seat again, discomforted. Men were dangerous, especially if you got their attention, and being interested in this one felt threatening somehow.

Yet she *was* interested, she couldn't deny it. What with those horrific scars and being Vasiliev's son-in-law, and the fact that he'd had a wife before her. And being a shadowy businessman that the press seemed to find frightening. Yet also the man who had freed her, who'd only reluctantly agreed to her marriage demand and who'd treated her with nothing but courtesy.

A puzzling man. A man of opposites and contrasts.

His expression was unreadable, those fascinating eyes of his glinting as he watched her.

Something about the way he was looking at her made her feel hot and restless. 'So, what?' With an effort she tried to keep her voice cool and not sound so impatient. 'Will you help me?'

'Get your friend away from Vasiliev, you mean? Yes, I will help.' He toyed with his champagne glass, his thumb rubbing against the stem.

'As it happens, I've already been gathering information on him. I will have to go through the proper legal channels in order to get Athena away from him permanently, so it might take some time. But she isn't in any immediate physical danger.'

The flutter in Rose's stomach fluttered even harder. So, he'd already been gathering information about Vasiliev. She hadn't expected that. He seemed not to care about anything much, yet... That wasn't quite true, was it?

'I understand,' she said. 'And thank you.' She tried not to give away the depth of her relief or how much that meant to her. 'I can give you—'

'No,' he interrupted calmly. 'You do not need to give me anything. I will help Athena and take down Vasiliev because it is the right thing to do. Nothing more and nothing less.'

She stared at him in surprise. Men, in her experience, were generally not concerned with doing the 'right thing.'

He stared back, enigmatic as a brick wall. Then he said, apparently reading her mind, 'What? Did you think I was like Vasiliev? I've already told you that I'm not.'

Her curiosity tightened. 'So, if you're not like him, then exactly what are you?'

He didn't reply immediately, his gaze falling to his glass for a moment. 'I was a soldier once, a long time ago,' he said at last. 'Then I became a businessman. Now I am building a legacy for someone who was concerned with injustice. Someone who was important to me.'

She had read that he'd been a soldier. A soldier in the French Foreign Legion.

What had happened to him? Was that where his scars had come from? Had he been burned in a military operation? And who was that someone he was talking about? The someone who'd been important to him?

She suspected she already knew—his first wife probably—but asking him about it would be taking her interest in him too far, which, again, might be dangerous.

Instead, she changed the subject. 'Why did you agree? To marry me, I mean?'

He took another leisurely sip of his champagne. 'I told you. I want children eventually. Heirs for my company and a family for myself. You were also rather…insistent.'

She ignored that. 'But why me? There must be lots of other women you could choose.'

He was silent, watching her the way he'd used to do back in that room in the compound, and she felt that awareness build between them once again. An awareness of each other that felt both exciting and dangerous at the same time. And she realised with a sudden lurch that he wasn't looking at her as if she was a servant, and he wasn't looking at her as if she was just another woman either.

He was looking at *her*. The person she was.

Then she realised something else. The enigmatic look on his face wasn't all that enigmatic, after all. Desire glittered in his eyes, along with curiosity, as if he found her just as fascinating as she found him.

Her mouth had gone dry, her heartbeat suddenly fast. Her skin prickled, a shivery, shimmery sensation, like a fine electrical field moving over her body.

'I think you know why I chose you,' Ares said softly. 'Tell me, little maid. Do you know what desire is?'

It was a simple question, the simplest, really, and she didn't know why it felt so charged. 'Desire?' She tried to keep her voice light, ignoring the 'little maid' thing. 'Of course. I was a prisoner. You think I didn't desire freedom?'

'I mean physical desire.'

Oh. She swallowed, trying to get some moisture into her suddenly dry mouth, and when that failed, she took another healthy sip of champagne. She didn't know why the question made her so uneasy.

'Yes,' she lied determinedly.

Ares gave her a look, then put his wine down and pushed his chair back. 'Come here.'

Rose narrowed her gaze. 'What?'

'I won't hurt you. I just want to show you something.' In the flickering light from the candles, his eyes gleamed silver. 'But if you're afraid, I won't force you.'

This was a manipulation, of course, challenging her to make her do exactly what he wanted. Yet she found herself powerless to resist. She was curious and she wanted to know what he was going to show her. Knowledge was power, after all.

Ignoring the sudden clutch of trepidation, Rose pushed back her chair. Got to her feet and moved around the side of the table, coming over to where he sat. And while the scared part of her wanted to keep some distance between them, the braver part, the warrior in her, insisted on coming closer. Standing right at the arm of his chair.

He remained still, his long, powerful body stretched out. And this close, even in the humidity of the night, she could feel his heat, as if that iron-hard body contained a furnace. She could smell him too, a delicious, woody, masculine spice.

She hadn't realised that she could like the heat of a man and his scent, and that it made her want to get closer, even though she knew she shouldn't.

'You are very beautiful,' he said quietly, staring up at her. 'Did you know that?'

She wasn't, though. Beauty had been valued in Vasiliev's house, but she certainly hadn't been. 'No.'

'Well, you are.' He lifted one hand and held it up to her in silent invitation.

His hand was large, long-fingered and strong-looking. There were scars on his fingers, old and white, standing out against his dark olive skin.

Rose's mouth was very dry. This shouldn't feel so scary. It was just a hand. He wasn't going to hurt her, he'd said, and she believed him. But she was conscious of a certain reluctance, as if touching him would change things, would start her off down a path she didn't want to go down. But still, this was a challenge, and she wasn't going to refuse it.

Slowly, she reached out and placed her hand in his.

His skin was hot, far hotter than she'd expected, and his palm was rough, his fingers callused. He might have been a businessman, yet his hands were those of someone who did hard, physical work.

It was shocking, this touch. She could feel that

electrical current ripple all over her skin, prickling down her spine, stealing her breath. And he watched her, his silver-green gaze unwavering as he slowly curled his fingers around hers.

His hand was so warm and so large, engulfing hers completely, containing it in a way that she thought might be threatening, yet it wasn't. It was reassuring, comforting even. But the way her own skin was prickling wasn't comfortable in the slightest.

Her heartbeat was very loud and very fast, and she wasn't sure why she was so short of breath. She stared at him, unable to look away, watching heat glitter in the depths of his eyes, and something shifted inside her, a fascination gripping tight.

The scars on his face extended down his jaw and the side of his strong neck, disappearing beneath the material of his white shirt, and suddenly she wanted to see how far down they went, maybe explore the differing textures of his skin. The rough and the smooth. He'd be hot, though, she knew that, and he'd feel hard, even where he was burned. Did they hurt him, those scars? If she touched them, would he feel it?

He stroked the back of her hand gently with one callused thumb, the roughness of it pulling over her skin and scraping just enough to send the most delicious shiver down her spine. What would that thumb feel like stroking other parts of her? More sensitive parts?

You know how it would feel. Amazing.

She took a ragged breath, caught in his silver-green gaze, a distant part of her urging her to pull her hand away, while the rest wanted her to leave it exactly where it was, enclosed in his.

After what felt like an endless stretch of time, the air around her feeling too hot and too close, he moved again, turning her hand over so it lay cupped in his, palm up, a pale starfish against his darker skin. Then everything in her tightened as he bent and pressed his mouth gently to the centre of her palm.

She gasped, unable to stop the sound as all the air rushed out of her, her whole body drawing tight. Her palm throbbed, and even as he lifted his head, she could still feel the impression of his mouth. It was as if he'd burned her.

His gaze was relentless, his expression unchanging. But it was his eyes that gave him away. There were flames in them and he let her see them.

An ache pulsed inside her, a deep, heaviness between her thighs, and she could feel the press of her sarong against her bare skin, the brush of it over her sensitive nipples. They felt hard, tight, and her breathing was far too fast.

She wasn't expecting it when Ares let her hand go, and she wasn't expecting not to want him to. She almost protested, but bit down on the words at the last second.

He only sat there watching her. 'That, little maid,' he said softly, 'is physical desire.'

She said nothing, her whole body alive and alight in a way it had never been before. Like Sleeping Beauty waking up, the world was different now and she didn't know what to say or what response to give.

Because if this feeling was desire, then she'd underestimated every single decision she'd made since she'd got here.

Sleeping with him will change you. Irrevocably.

Rose didn't know how or why, but she knew it was true all the same. It would change her. And it made everything she'd done so far, everything she'd planned for this evening, seem like the naive imaginings of a silly, sheltered girl.

She'd thought using his desire for her as a bargaining chip would give her power, but only because she hadn't understood what wanting him meant. She did now, though, and that left her vulnerable.

You can't sit here with him.

No, she couldn't. Suddenly it seemed like the most dangerous thing in the world.

Without a word, she turned around sharply and left him sitting on the terrace alone.

CHAPTER FIVE

Autumn

'I DON'T CARE,' Ares growled. 'Find her and find her now.' He hit the disconnect button, thrust his phone back in the pocket of his suit trousers, then turned from the window he'd been staring through and strode out of the study.

He'd arrived at his Cotswolds manor the night before, hoping to have some good news for Rose when she arrived today, but everything had gone to hell in a handcart, and he was in a foul temper.

The time had come for Rose to visit for her two weeks, and after what had happened in Thailand three months earlier, he'd decided to do things differently this time.

That summer he'd allowed himself to get too busy and had arrived a week late, not thinking about her in any particular way, only to find himself brought up short by a beautiful woman with a stubborn spirit and a blunt, fierce nature who'd somehow reached inside him and flicked a switch. A switch he'd had very firmly turned to 'off' for at least the last decade.

It shouldn't have mattered to him that she'd insisted on marrying him to pay back a debt. And he shouldn't have cared that she'd thought paying him with sex in return for freeing her friend was a perfectly valid choice.

He shouldn't have taken her small hand in his, intent on showing her that she'd lied and hadn't the first clue what desire had meant. And he definitely shouldn't have kissed her soft palm, making her turn on her heel and leave him sitting alone on the terrace.

Especially not when he'd known the night he'd taken her from Vasliev's clutches, the night she'd told him she'd marry him, that she had no idea at all what *any* of it meant. Not being a wife, not having children and definitely not a single thing about sex.

What had caused her to walk away, he wasn't sure. He hadn't hurt her, and he'd been very sure that the glitter in her wide golden eyes as he'd kissed her palm had been as much desire as it had been shock. She'd had a physical response to him, that was clear.

He'd wanted to follow her to ask her, but he also didn't want to force his company on her, so instead he'd kept his distance. If she wanted to talk, it would be her choice to come to him, but it was clear that she didn't want to talk since at the end of the week she'd left without even a goodbye.

He'd told himself it hadn't bothered him, but when he'd left himself, he couldn't deny a certain…disappointment.

He didn't often make missteps, but in this case, it seemed he had and that disturbed him. Naya would not have wanted him to upset Rose, but that night he'd kissed her hand, it hadn't been Naya he'd been thinking of.

All he'd wanted was to show her that it was a bad idea to go around offering herself to people without any clear idea of the implications or consequences. She was so inexperienced. Someone had to teach her.

However, the little lesson in desire he'd given her had frightened her in some way and he meant to find out why. And he'd also very much hoped to bring some good news with him this time too, to put at least some of her concerns about Athena to rest, yet that had just fallen through.

Athena had escaped Ivan's compound some months ago and no one knew where she was.

Since Thailand, he'd forwarded the information he'd collected on Ivan to the authorities, and they were now in the process of dealing with him. But Ares had wanted to secure Athena's freedom, then bring her to Rose personally. But that wasn't going to happen now, and he was in a foul mood about it.

You shouldn't be in any kind of mood, let alone an angry one.

That was true, he shouldn't. Which only added to his annoyance. Still, at least he had *some* news to give her, and that was better than nothing. She would be pleased to know Ivan was being handled at least.

He strode down the hallway of the little manor he'd bought on a whim five years ago. He had houses in many different countries since he liked to move around—staying in one place for too long made him restless—but this was the perfect location for an autumn meeting. The large oaks in the grounds had on all their autumn foliage and the rolling lawns were still green. There was a crisp bite to the air, and he thought Rose might enjoy rambling through the woods behind the manor.

She'd just arrived, and he'd instructed his butler who managed the house to show her into the library to wait for him. He wasn't going to let her sit and stew like he had in Thailand. He was going to show her around himself and maybe have a conversation about what had happened three months earlier.

He stopped outside the closed library door, suddenly aware of something else beneath the burn of his irritation. A sparking electricity, a kind of anticipation.

You've been looking forward to seeing her, don't deny it.

It was dangerous thing to admit, though. Certainly, he was looking forward to matching wills with her and having the same kind of blunt, honest conversations they'd had in Thailand. Plus, he liked the thick sexual tension that filled the air whenever they came into contact, a sexual tension she hadn't even been aware of until he'd made it obvious.

She is more sheltered than you thought.

No, it wasn't that she was sheltered, he suspected. It was that she *hadn't* been. Athena had protected her physically at the compound, but no one had protected her emotionally. She'd probably seen the worst men could do to women, and even if she hadn't experienced it herself, that would colour all her opinions of sex and desire.

He couldn't let his own desire goad him into making another slip like he had in Thailand. Nothing physical would happen between them, not until the year was up and she chose it. That was his bottom line.

He would need to go carefully.

Ares put his hand on the door handle and went in.

It was a warm, cosy little room, and his butler had made sure there was a fire burning in the fireplace. Tall wooden bookshelves lined the walls, a couple of worn but comfortable armchairs and a sofa set before the fire. Paintings of hunting scenes and forests were hung between the shelves, making the room feel very much like the house of an English aristocrat. Which he supposed was appropriate given that it had once belonged to an English aristocrat.

Rose herself stood before the fireplace with her back to him, her small hands outstretched to the blaze. The blue had faded completely from her hair, leaving its rich gold to gleam in the firelight. It was longer than it had been in Thailand, below her shoulder blades, and she had tied it back in a simple ponytail. She was dressed casually in jeans, a soft-looking jumper in stark black, with sneakers on her feet. A cheap black overcoat lay thrown over the back of the sofa.

He remained in the doorway a moment. He'd prepared himself, yet still the gut punch of desire made his breath catch.

How ridiculous. She wasn't in a bikini this time, and every inch of skin was hidden by her

clothing, yet all he wanted to do was to lay her
down on the hand-knotted silk rug in front of
the fire and peel those clothes off her, see what
her naked body looked like in the firelight. And
whether the rest of her was as golden and felt as
silky as her hand had that night on the terrace.

Her small fingers cupped in his palm. Her
skin so soft and fragile beneath his mouth as
he'd kissed her. The flicker of a flame in her
golden eyes…

She turned sharply and he heard her indrawn
breath as their eyes met. For some reason it felt
like no time at all had passed since he'd seen
her, and that they were on that terrace in Thailand still, her hand in his, the desire she hadn't
been able to hide alive in her eyes.

The desire he could see burning there now.

He'd shut the door hard and taken a couple
of steps towards her before he even knew what
he was doing.

Theos, *weren't you supposed to go carefully?*

Ares stopped himself just in time and from
the widening of her eyes it was clear that she'd
known exactly what he'd meant to do. She didn't
look afraid, but there was wariness on her face
all the same, as if he was a dangerous animal
and she wasn't sure which way he was going
to leap.

She should be wary. You were just about to pounce on her.

Yes, and he should know, better than anyone, the dangers of letting your own desires blind you. Of letting your heart dictate your actions.

He *had* to control himself.

Ares thrust his hands into the pockets of his trousers to keep them contained.

The pulse at the base of her throat, just above the neckline of her soft jumper, was racing. He could barely look away from it.

'Hello, Ares,' she said.

He hadn't been aware that he'd missed the sound of her voice until he heard it again, light, husky, feminine. She used to hum while she'd cleaned the fireplace in his room at Ivan's. He'd never recognised any of the songs, but he'd liked hearing them. He'd found it soothing.

He gritted his teeth, forcing a leash on his hunger. 'Hello, little maid. Welcome to the Cotswolds. I don't think you've been to England, have you?'

The soft curves of her breasts rose beneath her jumper as she took in a breath, and he couldn't look away from those either. 'No. But then you know that already, don't you?'

He did. He knew everything that she'd been doing since he'd made it his business to know. So, he knew that instead of traveling and seeing a bit more of the world, she'd stayed in Paris instead and worked at her job in the café. Chatted with her co-workers and went home every night to her little apartment.

There was no point denying it, so he didn't. 'Yes.'

'I thought so.' Her chin had that stubborn tilt to it again. 'There's a guy who sits in a car across the street from my cafe. Sometimes he comes in for a coffee, but most of the time he just sits in his car. Except of course when the time comes for me to go home.'

You really think she wouldn't notice? She's far too smart for that.

Perhaps he should have been annoyed that she'd spotted the member of one of his specialist teams that he'd sent to keep an eye on her, but he wasn't. The man was an expert at tailing people and yet still she'd seen him. He liked that. She was, indeed, far too smart.

'It is for your protection,' he said.

'Worried about the risk to your investment?' There was acid in her tone. So much for hoping she wasn't going to be angry with him. But was it only because she hadn't liked being watched or was there something more going on?

'You're my wife.' He met her challenging gaze head-on. 'I want you to be safe.'

'You also want to know exactly what I'm doing, don't you?'

He ignored that. 'Is it me having you watched that's really making you angry or was it what happened in Thailand?'

She stared at him for a second, then abruptly turned back to the fire, holding her hands out once more to the blaze. 'Nothing happened in Thailand,' she said after a moment.

Ares took a couple of steps closer. She was standing very rigidly, though he wasn't sure whether it was anger or fear that was making her so tense.

He couldn't leave it the way he had in Thailand. He needed to find out what was wrong.

'You walked away so abruptly,' he murmured. 'Then I didn't see you again for the entire week. I wanted to give you some space and I thought you might…come to me to discuss things, but you didn't.'

She said nothing.

He had no idea what she was thinking and suddenly that felt unacceptable. This was important. He needed to know if he'd made things difficult for her.

So, he took another couple of steps, closing the distance between them until she was mere inches away. He could see the rounded curve of one cheek, the flames from the fire sending golden flickers over her skin, and since her hair was pulled back and the neckline of her jumper low, he also noted the delicate arch of her neck, the fragile contours of her collarbones and the curve of one small ear. She had her ears pierced and wore small golden hoops.

Pretty. So pretty.

She must have sensed him standing behind her, because he could see how her shoulders tensed. Was that him making her uncomfortable? Was he standing too close?

He should move and yet… He didn't.

'Rose,' he said quietly into the silence. 'We will talk about this, understand me? I am not going to let you walk away a second time.'

Still, she said nothing, her gaze fixed on the flames in front of her, tension radiating from her.

'Rose.' This time he put an edge of command in his voice. 'Look at me.'

She didn't want to look at him. She didn't want him standing so close. She didn't want to be here with him. And she very much didn't want to feel the aching heaviness that sat deep inside her, or the crackling, spitting electricity that prickled over her skin the instant she'd seen him in the doorway.

For three months she'd told herself that her

response to him that night in Thailand had been an aberration, a trick of being somewhere new and exciting, and that once she left, once he wasn't in her vicinity, it would disappear.

Yet she hadn't been able to get him out of her head.

Ares sitting arrogantly in that chair, with his big, hard muscled body so close.

Ares cradling her hand in his, slowly turning it palm up and pressing his scarred mouth to it.

The memory of that mouth on her skin had haunted her, and even now, months later, she could still feel the burn of his kiss on her palm.

'This is desire.'

She hadn't known. She hadn't ever known what it was until he'd shown her. Until she'd realised what a fool she'd been, thinking to use sex against him, thinking it didn't matter. And that was the problem. She could feel the power of it inside her now and she knew it made everything different.

Because desire did matter. It did. It wasn't abstract any more, and while being in the outside world had certainly shown her that it was possible to want a man and that sex could be pleasurable, there was a part of her that had never quite believed it.

But she did now. She knew what it felt like to

want someone, and she hadn't liked how vulnerable it made her feel, not to mention stupid.

Stupid to have offered herself to him so many times without even the faintest clue about what it meant.

Facing him again after that night in Thailand had felt impossible, the power she'd thought she had an illusion. Wanting him had frightened her, because wanting anything had been a dangerous thing for a prisoner. She'd avoided him the whole rest of the week, which she supposed made her a coward, but she hadn't been able to process this new knowledge about herself with him around.

Rose swallowed. This was silly. He hadn't hurt her—he'd only kissed her palm, for God's sake—so why she was acting like the scared little girl she'd once been, she had no idea. She didn't want to be afraid. Not the way she had been back in the compound. Afraid and powerless, a victim.

No. Not again. Never *again.*

Gathering her courage, Rose turned around and met his gaze.

Instantly all the breath left her body.

She'd known he was standing behind her, she'd felt his heat, but she hadn't realised how close. Only inches away. And he towered over her. So tall, like a building or a tree, like one of the oaks she'd seen through the car window as they'd driven up to the manor. Huge, encompassing, his wide shoulders and muscled chest seemingly taking up the entire world. Before, in Thailand, he'd been sitting down and, apart from that one time as he'd stood beside the sun lounger, she hadn't understood just how tall he was or how that would affect her. One kiss in the palm of her hand had set her alight, but him standing so close, his body hotter than the fire at her back, the spicy, masculine scent of his aftershave all around her, was making her burn.

He wore another expertly tailored business shirt tonight, though this time in black and his suit trousers were also black. He seemed dark, powerful, the very epitome of who he'd been named for, the god of war, and that should have made her afraid, but it didn't.

His mesmerising silver-green eyes reminded her of olive leaves, so startling in his dark and scarred face, and she found herself staring up into them, her breath coming faster, shorter.

'I need to tell you something,' he said. 'I was hoping that since Ivan is being dealt with, I could also bring your friend Athena to you, but I just had news today that it appears she has already escaped.'

He'd emailed her a month earlier to tell her that steps against Ivan were being taken and that he was making enquiries about Athena, and she'd been so shocked that he was actually doing what he'd promised that it had taken her a good ten minutes to reply.

She'd felt helpless to do anything for her friend, and yet Ares, in one fell swoop, had not only brought Vasiliev to justice, but had maybe rescued Athena as well. Except, obviously, he'd been too late.

She swallowed, even now afraid to hope. 'Escaped? But…she's alive?'

'Yes.' There was a strange expression in his silvery-green gaze, one she couldn't immediately identify. 'It seemed she escaped a week before the authorities raided the compound.'

'She wasn't sold? She wasn't taken—'

'No. My sources told me that Ivan was furious, so it really was an escape attempt.' His expression remained as inscrutable as it always was, yet that there was a certain…softness in his eyes. 'I'm sorry I couldn't bring you better news. I had hoped to tell you she was safe and well and that you could see her. But I thought you'd want to know that she got out.'

That look in his eyes was concern, she suddenly realised. Concern for her. As if he cared what this news might mean for her and whether she would be upset.

And an odd feeling spread out inside her,

warmth shot through with sparks. No one had ever been concerned about her feelings. No one had ever been concerned for her at all.

No one except this hard, frightening man who apparently cared more than he let on.

That warm, sparking feeling pulsed lightly in her chest, and completely without conscious thought, Rose lifted a hand and touched his scarred and melted cheek.

His eyes widened and she knew a moment of intense satisfaction that she'd shocked him, then the look of concern vanished and something hungry and hot leapt in his gaze.

He lifted his own hand, his fingers closing around her wrist, gripping her firmly. She hadn't forgotten how hot his skin was, not one single iota, and if she'd had any breath left in her lungs, it would have burned away in that instant.

He left her hand where it was, resting on his cheek, but his hold was firm. She didn't know if that meant he wanted her to touch him or not. She still couldn't believe she actually was, but there was no backing away and she knew it.

She'd touched him. She'd crossed a line. And while she still felt vulnerable about wanting him, and afraid about what it would mean for her to go on touching him, she also didn't want to let that fear stop her. She didn't want to keep on being afraid.

He'd done something for her. He'd handed his own father-in-law to the authorities, had tried to find Athena for her. He'd been concerned for her feelings and she wanted to acknowledge that. Let him know that it meant something to her.

Yet at the feel of his burned skin beneath her fingertips, she was consumed by a sudden curiosity, intrigued by how some parts were shiny and smooth, while others were rough. All parts were hot, though, burning her fingertips, making the ache inside her get more intense. Making her breasts feel heavy and her sex throb.

This is desire.

She was breathing very fast, and she knew that maybe she'd made a mistake, that this was a bad idea, yet she couldn't stop, her fingers trailing down his twisted cheek to his hard, scarred mouth. It felt soft beneath her fingertips, so soft. The only thing about him that had any give.

'What are you doing, little maid?' His harsh, rasping voice had become even harsher, guttural almost.

She could barely speak. Her heartbeat was so loud she could barely hear him either, but she kept her fingertips on the softness of his mouth, tracing his lower lip. 'I just… Thank you for trying to help. That means a lot to me.'

His grip on her tightened, just shy of painful, yet he didn't pull her hand away. 'You do not owe me anything. I've told you that before.'

Rose swallowed. 'I know. I didn't mean it like that. It's just… I can't stop thinking about this. About you…' She dragged her gaze from her fingers and looked up his face. 'Will you show me?'

His fingers closed around her wrist in a convulsive movement, his grip now painful. But she didn't want to show any weakness, so she bit down on the pain. She'd told him she wasn't a doormat, and so she wouldn't be one.

His gaze was now all silver, tarnished and glittering in the firelight, and she could feel that thing crackling between them, that tension, glorious and electric.

Desire.

It didn't feel like a weakness now, not when she could see it burning so clearly in his eyes. He felt it too, didn't he?

'You need to be more specific,' he said, raw and guttural. 'I have not been with a woman in years, and I would…hate for there to be any misunderstandings.'

Shock echoed through her. She hadn't wondered about his love life, not once.

But he'd been married before and even with those burns he was phenomenally attractive.

Mesmerising, his presence a force of nature. She couldn't imagine him alone.

'Years?' she asked.

'Not since my wife died.' The words were bitten out, his big body full of tension, as if he was struggling with something. 'But you, little maid... *You*—' He broke off, but she didn't need him to elaborate. She already knew.

For years he hadn't been with anyone else, yet now he wanted her.

Her, the abducted girl no one had looked for and the servant no one thought about; she was wanted by this man. The god of war.

She wanted to ask him about his wife and how long he'd waited and why, and why her? Why now? But the heady rush of power that filled her couldn't be denied, and it felt different to the power she'd thought she'd had on that terrace in Thailand. Then it had only been an abstract concept, about her femininity, her body. Now, though, it was about *her*.

She was the one he wanted. Not just any woman, but her.

It mattered, she didn't know why, but it did, and that made her brave. Even braver than she'd thought she'd be.

Rose cupped his scarred cheek, ran her thumb along his lower lip. Then she went up on her toes and pressed her mouth to his.

He didn't wait, not one second. He pulled on her wrist, tugging her right up against him, and with his other hand resting firmly at the small of her back he held her there. And then he devoured her like a lion with his kill. Open, hot, hungry. His tongue was in her mouth, and she knew a moment's fear that she'd be swept away, caught in a riptide that was far too strong for her. But she only had two options now: either she pushed him away, or she surrendered.

She'd never thought she'd give up all control again, but there was no fighting this. And more, she didn't want to. She wasn't afraid any more. She wanted to go with the tide wherever it took her.

So, she curled her fingers into the fabric of his shirt and kissed him back.

She had no idea what she was doing; she'd never kissed anyone before. But for the past six months everything she'd done had been new and this was just one more new thing. One more glorious, amazing new thing.

His mouth was hot, soft and hard at the same time, demanding something of her that she didn't understand. But she answered that demand all the same, pressing herself against the hard wall of his chest, her tongue touching his as she tried to explore him the way he was exploring her. He made a hungry sound deep in his chest, and the hand at her back was like an iron bar, forcing her even closer to him.

Her entire front was plastered up against his and there was nothing but hardness everywhere. And he was hard. Like the oak tree she'd imagined, or no, harder. An iron figure of a man, unyielding in every way except his mouth.

She shuddered as he kissed her deeper, with a feverish intensity. He tasted of wine or chocolate or coffee, a dark, rich taste that made her realise how hungry she was. So hungry and she didn't even know it.

Then he pulled his mouth away, kissing down the side of her neck, making her tremble as he set his teeth against the sensitive cords there, nipping her so that she gasped aloud. Next, he found the pulse that beat at the base of her throat and kissed her, his tongue on her skin, and she felt like she would go mad if he didn't kiss her lower, run that incredible mouth of his all over her body.

'Ares,' she whispered hoarsely, even though she really didn't know what she wanted, only that she wanted more. 'Ares…'

The hand at the small of her back had somehow slid beneath the hem of her jumper, his rough, callused fingertips stroking her bare back since she wasn't wearing anything underneath it. And then his fingers moved higher, tracing each vertebra, sending the most delicious chills through her.

But she didn't want him to only touch her back, she wanted him touching her in other places, more sensitive places. Her breasts and between her thighs, yes, especially there.

'Rose,' he growled against her mouth. 'You must know that I was not planning on this. I was not planning on anything physical happening between us until you made the decision to stay married to me. So, if this is what you want, you had better be sure, because I do not think I can stop.'

For the first time she heard the lilt of an accent in his voice. An accent that felt familiar, as if she'd heard it somewhere before. He was Greek, that she remembered, and yet there had been no Greeks in the compound, so how could she have heard it before?

But then that thought was swept away as the grip on her wrist shifted and he was bringing her hand down to rest on his chest along with the other. He released her wrist only to grip her hips, fitting her more firmly against him so the soft, intense ache between her thighs was pressed to the long, hard ridge behind his fly.

'Rose,' he murmured again, more demanding this time. 'I need your agreement before this goes any further. It has been a long time and I do not think I can be gentle with you.'

She understood and again she wanted to know exactly how long it had been, but she didn't want to break this moment with questions. Not now she knew what she wanted and quite desperately.

In the compound she'd been alone. Nothing good had ever happened to her, nothing wonderful. There had been moments of lightness, when she'd spent time with Athena, but they'd been all too brief.

Until he'd walked into her world, and everything had changed. Thanks to him, she had Paris. Thanks to him, she had a job and an apartment. Thanks to him, she had freedom. She had justice thanks to him, and he'd tried to rescue her friend, and now he was giving her something else, something wonderful, and she wanted it so badly she thought she would die if she didn't have it.

'Yes,' she whispered, trembling against him. 'Ares, yes. Please.'

He didn't wait. One moment she was standing upright, held up against him, the next she was lying on her back on the silken rug in front of the fire with him kneeling astride her thighs, looking down at her.

The light from the flames flickered over his

scarred face, highlighting the deep twists and gouges of the scars, but she barely saw them. All she could see was the burning silver of his eyes as they looked down at her, avid and hungry, full of desire.

As promised, he wasn't gentle. He shoved the jumper she wore up under her arms, along with her plain black bra, exposing her breasts. Then he bent over her, his hot mouth closing around one sensitive nipple and sucking hard.

She gasped, the sensation so indescribably intense she could barely stand it. The heat of his mouth and the pressure were doing the most incredible things to her. She'd really had no idea at all that it would feel quite *so* good.

He sucked harder and her back arched as she thrust herself up into his mouth, wanting more of this pleasure, this intense sensation, the dragging ache between her thighs becoming more and more insistent.

She lifted her hands, but he gripped her wrists and pressed them flat to the floor on either side of her head, holding them there as he transferred his attention to her other breast, his teeth against her nipple, biting gently and sending yet more sparks cascading everywhere. The feeling of being restrained made the pleasure somehow sharper, except she wanted to touch him.

She wriggled, trying to free her wrists. 'Please, Ares…'

He made a growling sound against her breast, releasing her nipple and raising his head. His gaze was all fire, all sharp intensity. 'What is it?' His voice was stone on stone, grating together. 'Am I hurting you?'

'No,' she panted, trying to get her voice working. 'I just…want to touch you. I want to see you.'

He stared at her for a second, then abruptly released her wrists and sat back on his knees again. Keeping his gaze fixed to hers, he lifted his hands and undid the buttons of his shirt, pulling it open.

The breath left her body and she stared, unable to help herself. The whole left side of his body was scarred, as if he'd been licked by fire, chest and shoulders and abdomen all twisted, melted flesh. Like his face, some parts were shiny, and some were rough, white and stark against the bronze of his skin. But even beneath the scars, she could see the carved outlines of muscles that look like they'd been chiselled from stone. The contrasts of him were beautiful to her in a way she'd never expected.

She sat up, reaching for him, touching the smooth olive skin of the unburned part of his chest, then running her fingers over some of the tightened scar tissue. All parts of him were so hot she felt burned herself.

He looked like he'd been created in a forge where the heat was so intense that even his skin hadn't been able to withstand the fire. But his bones and his muscles had, the fundamental part of him was granite hard.

He said nothing as she touched him, his hands dropping to his belt and undoing it. He flicked open the buttons of his trousers, before pulling down the zip of his fly. She could hear his breathing, it was as ragged as hers, and beneath her hand she could feel the beat of his heart. Fast, powerful.

Again, he didn't speak as he pushed her back down again, his hands at the buttons of her jeans, pulling at them, undoing them. Then he was jerking down the denim to the tops of her thighs, taking her underwear with them, and somehow the fact that he didn't undress her entirely or himself, was intensely erotic. As if he couldn't wait.

A curse escaped him as he looked down at her, all exposed for him, in a language that was at once foreign to her and familiar at the same time. And a dim part of her tried to puzzle it out, but then he was jerking at the denim, shifting as he spread her thighs so he could kneel between them. Positioning himself, and then stretching over her. And she could feel the hot, hard length of him pressing against her entrance, then sliding in slowly. Deep and then getting deeper.

She groaned. He felt big and it hurt, but it was a good pain. She didn't want him to stop. Strange tears started in her eyes, and then suddenly it didn't hurt any more and there was only him, filling her so completely that she hadn't known she'd been empty until this moment. She hadn't known that she'd ever wanted someone there, but she had. She'd wanted him. He was still for a moment, the blazing intensity of his gaze looking down into hers, and she felt her body adjust. He fit her like he'd been made for her.

Then he began to move, and everything became desperate, the ache inside her building until she didn't think she could bear it. Yet she wanted more, because even though the friction was driving her mad, it somehow wasn't enough.

She twisted beneath him, her hands against his bare chest, her nails digging in, heedless of his scars. 'Ares,' she gasped. 'Ares... More. Please...'

His mouth took hers, her desperate pleas lost, and then his hand was down between her thighs, his fingers applying the most exquisite pressure right where she needed it most. Then he gave one hard thrust and she felt as if the whole world was coming apart and her right along with it.

Dimly, in the corner of her mind that wasn't quite lost, she was conscious of his own movements, faster, harder. Then he gave a low, guttural roar, before he joined her, lying in pieces before the fire.

CHAPTER SIX

ARES LAY THERE for a full minute, completely and utterly stunned. He hadn't expected this to happen, not any of it. He'd thought she'd be upset when he'd told her about Athena, not that she'd touch his face and kiss him. And he certainly hadn't expected her to then turn so soft and hot in his hands that he hadn't been able to resist her.

He hadn't expected to pull her down onto the rug in front of the fire, to be so lost that he hadn't even bothered to undress her properly, his only thought to get inside her as quickly as possible.

What he'd expected was another six months of her getting to know him and mastering his own desire until—*if!*—she decided she wanted to remain married to him.

What happened to your control? You didn't even bother to use protection.

He gritted his teeth, trying not to be furious

with himself as well as ignoring the odd possessiveness at the thought of her being pregnant with his child.

He'd promised Naya children and he'd meant to provide them, and he'd honestly thought he'd be more detached about the idea of having children with someone else and yet… He wasn't quite as detached as he'd thought he'd be.

You weren't supposed to touch her. You were supposed to wait.

The fury at himself twisted tighter, but he shoved it away. It was too late to get wound up about it now. She'd touched him and it was he who'd gone up in flames. He'd let himself go too long without a woman, let himself be overcome by desire and by the look in her eyes when he'd told her about Athena, as if he'd handed her the moon and the stars on a plate, and every single one of his controls had vanished.

He had no one but himself to blame for it. He had to do better.

He lifted his head and looked down at her.

Rose's face was flushed, small tendrils of hair that had escaped her ponytail clustered around her damp forehead in tiny threads of gold. Her eyes were very wide, staring at him, the firelight gilding the tips of her lashes.

She looked just as shocked as he felt.

'Are you all right?' His voice sounded even

rougher than it normally was. 'I hurt you.' It wasn't a question. He'd felt her tense as he'd pushed inside her. And he'd tried to stop then, but…

It had been years. *Years.* The feel of her, the heat of her, the scent of her body and the sounds she'd made, everything so soft and silky and smooth…

He'd forgotten how incredible it felt to sink into a woman's body, to feel her clench around him, to hear her sighs in his ears as he gave her pleasure. To feel her welcome him and enclose him…ah, *Theos*, how could he have forgotten all of that?

Perhaps he'd denied himself too long and that was why it had been so good. He just missed sex. Nothing to do with Rose in particular.

'It hurt a little bit. But not really.' She was staring at him as if she'd never seen anything like him in all her life. 'Ares…is it always like that?'

He liked that expression on her face. It made everything male in him, the parts of himself he'd almost forgotten, growl with satisfaction. 'Not always,' he said roughly, remembering the first few fumbling times before he'd met Naya.

He shifted slightly so he wasn't lying on top of her, realising as he did so that he was getting hard again, and that he didn't want to push himself away from her completely. What he wanted was to strip her clothes off her, feast on her naked body until he had her screaming, and then he wanted to be inside her again, feeling the tight clasp of her sex around his, moving inside her until they both lost their minds.

Except that losing his mind had never been part of his promise to Naya. Children, he'd promised her, nothing more. Then again, it was just physical pleasure, that's all, and certainly nothing lasting.

Enjoying sex with Rose didn't mean anything.

'What is it?' she asked, a crease between her brows, obviously noticing his abstraction. 'I'm sorry. I shouldn't have kissed you—'

He laid a finger across her mouth to silence her, because it hadn't been her that had been the problem. 'Kissing me is exactly what you should have done.' He removed the finger. 'I'm only sorry that it was so quick. I had intended our first time to be...different.'

The crease between her brows deepened. 'You said you haven't...been with anyone since your wife died...?'

Instantly he tensed. He didn't want to talk about this, not now, but he owed her an explanation for why he'd been so rough. Especially when she hadn't deserved it.

'No,' he said.

Rose hesitated a moment, then asked, 'I know it's none of my business, but…how long? You said years.'

'Yes, it has been years.' He knew he'd sounded sharp, but he hoped she'd got the message that he wasn't up for a conversation about this now. Perhaps one day he'd tell her about Naya, but not now. Not today.

'Oh,' she said softly, her big golden eyes searching his face, looking for what he didn't know, but he could see she had more questions. 'Ares,' she went on. 'How were you burned?'

He didn't want to answer that one either, not given how linked that subject was with Naya.

'I only ask,' she continued quickly, 'because I wasn't sure if it was okay to touch them or whether they hurt you or…'

It's a valid question. She should know if you want her to stay married to you.

No, she shouldn't. And he wasn't even sure he wanted her to stay married to him himself. Regardless, knowing wasn't necessary for the getting of heirs. She didn't need to know about his wife or the circumstances that lead to her death. About his pride and the hard lessons he'd had to learn.

About your failure.

Yes, that too.

Her past was shrouded in mystery, they didn't

and couldn't talk about hers, so why should he have to reveal his? That wasn't her fault admittedly, but still.

'You can touch the burns,' he said shortly. 'They don't hurt. Some places have no sensation because the nerve endings have burned away, so I might not feel it if you touch me there.'

She was silent a moment, clearly waiting for him to elaborate, but he didn't.

A flicker of emotion passed over her face. 'I'm sorry, I shouldn't have asked.'

'Rose,' he began.

But then she touched the side of his face again, where the scar tissue was thick and twisted. He couldn't feel her fingertips, but he knew they were there, and something shuddered in his chest. 'Thank you for showing me about…desire,' she said. 'But I wonder…could we possibly explore the subject more?'

He was glad that was the subject she wanted to pursue and not anything else. More sex might be a mistake, but he was getting hungrier by the moment, conscious of how soft and warm her body was, and the scent of sweet feminine arousal heavy in the air around him.

Yes, he had missed sex and he wanted it. What was the point in holding back now?

'We could,' he said, shifting once again, going back onto his knees. His hands dropped to the hem of her jumper. 'But understand, Rose. If you want this, if you want me, you cannot go back.' He stared down into her eyes, so she could see the intention in his. 'You are the only woman I have wanted since my wife died, and if you cross this line with me now, I will want more.'

For a second, she only stared back. 'Why me?' she asked suddenly. 'What's so special about me? I'm just a girl you bought from your father-in-law. A girl who doesn't even know her real name. Why should I be the only woman you've wanted?'

He'd only alluded to the truth the last time she'd asked. But she deserved more than that from him now.

'Because regardless of who you really are, regardless of your past, we have chemistry. And because, little maid, even though you grew up in a terrible place, you are fearless. A warrior through and through.' His fingers tightened in the soft wool. 'Or am I wrong?'

The gold of her eyes glowed bright and he had the sense he'd just given her something she liked. A gift that she'd needed. He liked that, but it also made him want to ask her why being fearless, why being a warrior, was so important to her.

Except then she lifted her arms up in wordless invitation and all the thoughts vanished from his head.

Ares jerked her jumper up and over her head, then tore her bra off. She made no move to stop him or cover herself, her gaze never leaving his face, a fierce expression on hers.

No, he wasn't wrong. She *was* a warrior.

He shifted so he could take the rest of her clothes off, so she was finally lying on the silken rug in front of the fire the way he'd fantasised about: naked. And she didn't move as he leaned over her, bracing himself with one hand beside her head so he could pull out the tie of her ponytail and spread her golden hair out all around her.

Then he just looked at her. Looked at her for a long, *long* time. Because it had been years since he'd had a naked woman stretched out beneath him, ready for him and wanting his touch. A woman all gleaming and gilded, painted in shades of gold by the fire. Warm skin, silken hair, molten eyes. All for him.

She was flushed and her nipples were hard, and she didn't look away. So many people couldn't bear to look at him, a man scarred and ruined and harder than iron. A pitiless man. A man whose heart had died in a fire long ago.

She wasn't afraid of that man. She had never been afraid of that man. And she didn't need gentleness from him, or tenderness. She didn't need him to be careful, because she was strong enough to take anything he could throw at her.

And as if to prove it, she reached up and thrust her fingers into his hair and pulled his mouth down on hers.

This kiss was hotter than the one she'd given him just before and hotter than the one he'd returned. Hotter even than the flames in the grate. Raw and wild, a firestorm.

He kissed her back without restraint, just as hungry, ravaging her mouth, gorging himself on the taste of her, mint and strawberries and something else sweet. Then he took her bottom lip between his teeth and nipped her hard, drawing a gasp from her and making her fingers tighten in his hair. And he didn't stop there.

He moved down her body, kissing the stubborn line of her jaw and the graceful arch of her neck, the pulse that beat at her throat—he concentrated on that for quite a while—before moving down to the lush curves of her breasts. He nipped and sucked on each one, even as his hands moved over her, relishing her softness and the silky feel of her warm skin. She twisted and shifted the lower he went, every touch of his mouth drawing tortured gasps and soft little pleas.

He liked that too much and when she tried to

sit up, her hands reaching for him, he pressed a hand to her stomach and held her down, because he wasn't finished. Not by a long stretch. Then finally he settled between her spread thighs and touched the softness between them, all slick and hot, making her writhe with his fingers and then, because he was desperate to taste her, his mouth.

It had been too long since he'd done this too, touched and tasted a woman, taken his time building her pleasure. He'd forgotten how hard it had made him, how like a god he felt when she pleaded for release.

He'd perfected the art of violence, knew a hundred different ways to kill a man. Had built a billion-dollar company in the space of fifteen years, yet he hadn't realised, until right this minute, how all of that had been for someone else. For Naya.

He hadn't had anything for himself. Yet this woman beneath him, Rose, she was his. Tonight, in this moment, she was utterly and completely his.

Perhaps it was wrong to be glad of that so savagely, but he let himself have it.

He let himself glory in the sweetness of her, and she was so very sweet, the taste of her heady as any drug. She cried out as he pushed his tongue inside her, exploring her slowly and with great relish, his hands firmly pressing down on her thighs so she couldn't move. So, he had her exactly where he wanted her. And he took his time, because it had been so long, and her cries were music to his ears, the shudder and shift of her hips a dance he'd never tire of.

And as he brought her finally to the edge and pushed her off it, amid her cries of pleasure, he knew that he wouldn't be able to bear any more distance between them.

This was how it would be from now on and he would brook no argument.

Rose stared at the ceiling and tried to determine how she could put herself back together again since she was pretty sure Ares had shattered her into little pieces. Not that she cared. She could lie here like this for ever, the effects of that orgasm pulsing through her, pleasure glittering like a net of sparks laid over her skin.

She'd had no idea she could feel so intensely, that her body could give her so much ecstasy, and all it had taken was his rough hands and his wicked mouth on her. It might have been years since he'd done that, but it was clear that he'd either been born with a gift or whatever lessons he'd learned about how to please a woman he'd forgotten none of them. And he'd practiced a *lot*.

Yes, of course he did. With his first wife.

A small, edged kind of feeling wound through her at the thought, like the needle-fine and sharp edge of a bit of paper, cutting at her, but she ignored it. Now wasn't the time to be thinking about his first wife, not with him suddenly rearing above her, still mostly clothed and his shirt open.

He knelt and reached for her hips, hauling her up and over his hard thighs, her legs spread on either side of his waist. And he gripped her firmly as he pushed himself inside her. She shuddered, the net of sparks pulling tight, sensitive tissues stretching with the most exquisite burn. She closed her eyes as he moved, long and deep, her entire world narrowing to the heat of him inside her, beneath her, holding her fast.

His hands were red-hot brands on her hips, and it felt as if he was imprinting himself on her, leaving scorch marks. Turning every part of her into flame.

It was so intense, so wonderful, she didn't think she could bear it. But she was a warrior, wasn't she? That's what he'd called her, that's what he'd said. That's why he wanted her, because she was a warrior, a fighter, not a victim and not a servant. Not a passive woman waiting for her next instruction, too scared to leave her prison.

As the pleasure climbed between them, Rose opened her eyes and put her hands over his where they gripped her and pulled herself up so she was sitting upright in his lap. His tarnished silver eyes were right in front of her, the iron-hard plane of his chest pressed against the softness of her breasts.

He didn't stop, he kept on moving, and she didn't stop either. She moved with him, watching the signs of pleasure chase over his scarred face, because she knew what to look for now. The lines around his eyes tightening, the powerful cords of his neck standing out, his mouth hard. The fire leaping and blazing in his eyes.

She gripped his shoulders, dug her nails in, and they moved together, building the pleasure between them so sharp, so acute, she was trembling. Then he pushed his hand down between them for that sweet extra friction and she was shattering once again, his name a scream gathering in her throat. But his mouth covered hers, swallowing the scream as she felt his big body thrust once and then again, hard and deep. Then his arms were around her, crushing her against him, holding her as he roared out his own release.

For long minutes afterwards, he held her like that, and she didn't want to move. Her head was resting on his hard, scarred shoulder, while one of his hands had buried itself in her hair. His arm was like iron around her waist, and she could hear the beat of his heart, loud and strong and steady.

She drifted a few moments, her thoughts returning to what he'd told her earlier, about the burns, and about what he hadn't said too. He hadn't mentioned how he'd got them, and she thought it was deliberate. He hadn't forgotten her question, he'd just chosen not to answer it, though she could guess why.

It had something to do with his wife, she was sure. Perhaps those burns had happened at the same time she'd died. Perhaps their home had burned down, and he'd got out and his wife hadn't.

Or he got them trying to save her.

Her heart felt tight, as if someone had pinched it suddenly and hard. On the surface he seemed impassive as stone, but just now he'd betrayed a passion and a possessiveness that ran deep. If he'd loved his wife with the same intensity of feeling, then of course he would have tried to save her.

Yet something had gone wrong, and she'd died.

That must cause him a great deal of pain.

The pinch around her heart became more acute. No wonder he didn't want to talk about it and no wonder he hadn't been with anyone else. If he'd tried to save her and failed, that must have been…devastating.

Before she knew what she was doing, she'd turned her head slightly and pressed a kiss to the scarred skin beneath her cheek, her heart aching. She wouldn't push him about this. She had no experience with grief—she hadn't ever lost a person like that. She hadn't ever had a person to lose, but that was beside the point. She didn't know anything about normal human experiences and could offer him no advice. All she had was the comfort of her body, and if he wanted that, then he could have it.

It would be her pleasure—literally.

His hand tightened in her hair, pulling her head up gently, his gaze moving over her, assessing her. 'Everything okay?'

'Yes.' She smiled, giving in to the heady feeling of being drunk on sex and on him. 'Everything is fantastic.'

His hard mouth softened a moment, amusement flickering in his silver-green eyes. But then both were gone, his expression implacable once again. 'First thing, little maid, is that I didn't use any protection.'

A shock went through her. Protection, of course. She hadn't even thought about it.

You could end up being pregnant. Already.

Her muscles tightened as a strange shiver went through her. And it wasn't dread. What would it be like to have a child? *His* child?

You have no idea how to be a mother. You don't even remember your own.

'Second thing,' he said before she could speak, 'no, I didn't plan on not using a condom the first time. Or the second time either. I wanted us to have more discussion about the subject. However...' His eyes glinted. 'It seems my control where you're concerned isn't as good as I'd thought.'

She swallowed, the warm glow of orgasm fading, something colder taking its place. She didn't remember her own mother, that was true. And she had no idea what being a mother even entailed, just as she had no idea about being a wife. Every time she thought she knew what was going on, something would happen to show her that she didn't, that she was still that ignorant, scared servant girl he'd rescued. The girl who didn't even know her real name.

'I see.' Her own voice sounded small and colourless in the warmth of the room. 'And what if I am pregnant? What will that mean for the year you promised me? Does it mean I don't get to choose? Will we have to stay married?'

His gaze narrowed, became sharp, a storm-tossed silvery sea. 'If you're pregnant we will be keeping the child, understand?'

There was a fierce undertone in his voice, a note that vibrated just on the edge of fury, though she didn't think it was directed at her. Whatever it was, though, it shocked her. Because when he'd mentioned children before, he'd done so very casually and in conjunction with bloodlines, rather than out of any desperate desire.

'Yes,' she said sharply. 'But that's not what I asked.'

His gaze flickered and the ferocity seemed to die out of his eyes. 'Apologies, little maid.' His voice was softer this time, yet no less rasping. 'I didn't mean to be quite so…vehement.'

And now she wanted to know why he was so 'vehement,' especially when he hadn't been so before, but then he went on. 'There is no need to discuss it now, not when we do not know if you even are pregnant. We can cross that bridge when we come to it.'

Briefly she debated pushing him for more of a plan, but then decided to let it go. She was relaxed and warm and sated, and so was he, and she didn't want to ruin the moment with an argument. Besides, she liked being held against him like this. She'd never been held before, and it made her feel safe. As if here in his arms, nothing could touch her, nothing could take her.

'It's okay,' she murmured, running her fingers over his chest. 'I shouldn't have been so sharp. It's only... I've only had six months of freedom and... Well. Call it cold feet.'

Again, there was a slight softening around his eyes and his mouth. The hand in her hair shifted, so he was cradling the back of her head, his fingers pressing lightly yet firmly against her skull in a way she found pleasurable. 'I can understand that. But should we end up having a child, it would not necessarily mean you'd be tied down.' His mouth curved. 'I am, after all, very rich and can afford any number of staff to help with its care.'

Its care...

Her stomach lurched again, the cold sensation returning. She had never felt her lack of past so acutely. She had no medical records, no family history... What if she passed on some terrible illness to her child that she hadn't even known she had?

She turned her head away, trying to hide her reaction, because she didn't want to talk about that. She didn't even want to think about it, but the long fingers cradling the back of her head firmed, keeping her in place. His gaze speared through her, pinning her. 'What is it?'

He wouldn't let her not answer, that was clear, and she supposed she might as well talk about it. After all, in a month's time she could already be pregnant. This was what being married was all about, wasn't it? Discussions about children.

Rose swallowed. 'I don't know who I am, Ares. I don't have a mother. I don't have anyone. No family history. What if I'm a carrier for some awful disease? And what kind of mother am I going to be when I can't even remember my own?'

He lifted one shoulder as if it didn't matter. 'You will be a perfect mother. You're a warrior, I told you that, which is exactly the kind of mother I want for our child. And as to your past, well, we will find out.'

He said it like it was already a foregone conclusion. As if *all* of this was a foregone conclusion. As if they already had children and they'd found out who she was, and it was easy and not a problem in the slightest.

None of this was what you thought it would be. None of it.

She had chosen to marry him, it was true. She was the one who'd demanded it. Yet had it been something she'd have insisted on if she'd known what it truly meant? That she would end up here, lying in his arms, aching with feelings she didn't quite understand?

The unprotected sex had been stupid of her. Because sure, while he might have taken responsibility for that, it went both ways. She was a virgin, but she'd done her research over the past three months. She knew what condoms were. She could have stopped him and demanded he put one on, but she hadn't. She'd been as lost to what was happening between them as he'd been.

Yet another thing you didn't know that you didn't understand.

But that thought wasn't a useful one. Right now, she was in his arms, and he was hot, and he felt good against her. And she wanted more of his heat, more of his passion. She wanted to explore him as thoroughly as he'd explored her, see if she could make him tremble, make him call her name. Exert her feminine power over him, bring him to his knees.

Yes, that's what she wanted.

She stared into his eyes, relaxing against him, her fingertips stroking his hard muscled chest, glorying in the feeling of being surrounded by his heat and his power. 'So, what about now? What do you want to do now?'

His mouth curved deeper, his attention dropping down to her throat and her breasts pressed hard to his chest. 'I think you can guess what I want.' He lifted his gaze back to hers. 'But it has to be what you want too. If not, then no matter what I told you earlier, you can walk away.'

Something fluttered hard behind her ribs, an unexpected emotion tightening in her throat.

It was as if he'd somehow known all the doubts about understanding and choices that had been going through her head. It was as if he knew her, and not just as the stranger he'd married or the trafficked woman he'd married, but her. Rose. Knew what she'd be thinking about now and what would distress her. She didn't know how he knew since they hadn't had much to do with each other these past six months, nevertheless he knew.

And perhaps it wasn't a good thing. Perhaps it was dangerous to be known in that way, yet it didn't feel dangerous. It felt reassuring. Comforting. She had always been a mystery to everyone including herself, a mystery that no one had ever wanted to get to the bottom of. But he had.

A warrior, he'd called her, as if he could see her soul already. And she liked it.

A warrior was exactly what she wanted to be.

So, she stared back at him and let him see her fierce spirit in her eyes. 'What happens is that you will take me up to your bed and you'll let me do whatever I want with you. And then in the morning, since it's only fair, you can do the same to me. And then after that, we'll start all over again.'

His smile widened and those silver-green eyes of his warmed, the green deepening, becoming less an arctic sea than a tropical one, making her catch her breath at his beauty. At the warmth of his smile and the scars that pulled at his skin, all melted and twisted and yet a part of him. She still didn't know why he had them, though she suspected, but they were beautiful too in their way, because they were part of him.

Again, this is dangerous. You shouldn't be thinking of him like that.

But she didn't know why it was dangerous to admire him, and she didn't want to think about it now. What she wanted was him and his smile, his beauty and his passion. She wanted the warrior in her to do battle with the warrior in him. A sensual battle full of pleasures she could only dream of.

'In that case, little maid,' he said softly. 'I think I can definitely accommodate you.'

Then she was caught up in his arms as he got to his feet and took her up to his bedroom. And as the afternoon descended into night, a fiery, hot, feverish night, one thing stayed stuck in her head. That this time she'd understood fully what she'd chosen downstairs in his arms, to have this moment, this night, with him.

And she had no regrets.

CHAPTER SEVEN

'No,' ARES SAID. 'Your hand needs to be like this.' He took Rose's small fist in his, extracted her thumb and tucked it over her clenched fingers, then he turned it so her knuckles were facing up. 'Then when you strike, you twist your arm like so.' He demonstrated, extending her arm, then turning it.

She watched him with unwavering focus, as if this was the most important thing she'd ever done, which was the way she approached most things, as he'd discovered.

They were in his gym at the manor, and he'd been teaching her some self-defence. He had a protection detail watching her in Paris, of course, but he'd thought it prudent to teach her how to defend herself. She'd been very keen to learn. In fact, she was very keen to learn about everything.

She was a quick learner too, never had to be told anything twice, and was stubborn when she didn't get it right the first time, trying and trying until she had it. The lessons he'd particularly enjoyed had been the ones he'd given her in bed, though after that first night, where he'd taught her all the ways in which to pleasure him, they'd discovered a few more things together and those had been particularly sweet.

He had to admit that he couldn't get enough of those lessons, as if all the long passionless years had created a need in him that couldn't be quenched by a couple of nights. Or even a couple of weeks. He was already wondering what he was going to do when her two weeks was up, and she went back to Paris. It would mean three months of celibacy for him and everything in him roared with denial at the thought of it.

Even right now, as she created the fist he'd taught her, that look of fierce concentration on her face, he could feel the burn of desire.

It's not just about desire, though, is it? You want to spend time with her.

He liked her, it was true, and he liked spending time with her. But this desire had nothing to do with that. It was completely and utterly physical.

Today Rose wore tight-fitting black yoga pants and a black athletic bra, her lush curves and golden skin on full display, and already he was imagining laying her down on the mat they stood on and pinning her there with his body, getting her to fight him until she finally surrendered in the most sensual of ways.

Maybe he would once he'd finished with their lesson. He didn't see why he couldn't indulge himself, not when she wanted it as badly as he did.

'Now,' he said. 'Punch me.' Her gaze flickered, a smile curving her mouth, and he grinned. 'Bloodthirsty, little maid. You don't need to look quite so pleased at the prospect.'

Her smile deepened and then her fist came out at speed. But he was still ex-Legion and he blocked it easily enough.

She sniffed, obviously dissatisfied with her performance. 'I want to try again.'

Ares released her fist. 'I've had years of experience at this, Rose. You've had all of an hour. You won't hit me if I don't want you to.'

She readied herself, elbows bent, her fists tight and drawn back at her sides. 'What experience? You were a soldier you said.'

'I was in the French Foreign Legion, spent years fighting in Africa.'

'Yes, I read about that. It's—'

'Not as romantic as it sounds,' he interrupted, because it hadn't been. War wasn't romantic. It was blood and desperation and fear and death, and there was nothing romantic about any of that. Not that it had been romance he'd wanted. He'd wanted escape from grief, pure and simple.

'Why?' She'd straightened a little, her curiosity caught. 'What made you join up?'

This was edging into territory he didn't want to get into, but it was inevitable the topic would rear its ugly head. And given that the purpose of these two weeks with each other was to get to know one another, it seemed churlish not to tell her. Besides, those years in the Legion where his life had boiled down to eating, sleeping, patrolling and obeying orders without question had been good years. Simple years. He hadn't had to think. His pain and suffering had only been physical, and he'd embraced it, pushing himself to his physical limits and beyond. He'd wanted to stay there for ever, but a bullet wound and difficulties with his burn injuries had prevented him.

'I joined because I wanted to test myself.' He reached for her fist again and adjusted it. 'My burns had healed but I wanted to get stronger, both physically and mentally, and the Legion seemed like a good fit.' Not exactly the truth, but not a lie either.

'What about the regular army?' Her gaze was on him as he adjusted her thumb. 'You were born in Greece, weren't you? So why didn't you go into the Greek army?'

'Because I didn't want to be in Greece. And the Legion takes men from every country.'

There was a crease between her brows. 'So why did you leave?'

'I was wounded in action in French Guiana and had some issues with the burn injuries, so that was my military career over.' The hospital there had been badly equipped and poorly staffed, and he'd suffered a post-surgical infection. They'd given him the last morphine they'd had, but that had been worse than the pain, causing him nightmares of burning buildings and hearing Naya calling for help, and him trying to batter down a door that wouldn't budge…

Your fault. Your failure.

He shoved the thought away and stepped back. 'Again.'

Rose's fist came out, faster this time, but still he blocked it easily.

She made an annoyed sound. 'So, is that when you started building your company?'

Another difficult subject. Still, he could give her some half-truths. 'I liked the Legion. Life was simple in it. And after I got out of hospital and realised my military career was over, I decided to recreate my own private military, so to speak.'

Rose was readying herself again, though her gaze was still fixed on him, curiosity burning bright in her beautiful eyes. 'Is that what Hercules Security is? I couldn't find much about it online.'

He grinned. 'You researched me?'

Colour stained her cheeks, which he found he liked very much. 'You're my husband and I didn't know anything about you. So yes, I looked.'

'You wouldn't have found much.'

'Hardly anything,' she agreed. 'Apart from Ares, God of War.'

He snorted. 'A stupid name. But no, there isn't much because my clients do not like publicity when it comes to military matters.'

'So…what do you do exactly?'

'We provide services to governments who cannot use their own military for various reasons, as well as helping out in times of civil unrest or natural disasters. There was an earthquake in China a month ago, for example, and I provided a team to help with digging survivors out of collapsed buildings.'

She frowned. 'But what does "services to governments" mean? Do you kill people they don't like or something?'

Anger shifted inside him at the note of censure in her voice and the hint of disapproval in her golden eyes.

He shouldn't let it get to him, but his company

was Naya's memorial, her legacy, and she'd be proud of what he'd accomplished, all the people he'd helped. It was not for Rose to judge.

'No,' he said, more terse than he'd intended. 'There are times when governments cannot be seen to intervene in a country's problems but need to in order to protect people. We help rescue citizens, protect civilians and try to contain dictators. Protecting the innocent is our aim, so do not be so quick to judge.'

Rose scowled. 'Well, how was I to know any of that? All I have to go on are a few articles on the internet that don't say anything, because you don't talk about yourself.'

She has given an awful lot of herself to you, while you have given her nothing.

All his muscles had gone tight, and he was very conscious of a defensive anger that he didn't want coiling inside him, along with a deeper guilt that he also didn't want.

Mainly because it was true.

'I did not think you would be interested,' he lied, trying to ignore both the anger and the guilt, and failing. 'Why I built my company doesn't matter anyway.'

But she didn't back down, because of course she wouldn't. 'Of course I'm interested. You're my husband and I want to know about you.

Wasn't that the whole point of spending two weeks with you every season?'

Ares scowled, the anger inside him gathering tighter and for no discernible reason. He didn't understand why his usually perfect control was frayed as old rope. So she'd got a little closer to the subject of Naya than he was comfortable with, and now she was pushing him harder for answers. So what? He could ignore it, couldn't he?

'My past is irrelevant,' he said curtly. 'For your purposes, all that matters is that my company makes me a lot of money. Money that you are enjoying right now.'

Sparks glittered in her eyes. 'I don't want your money, Ares. I never asked for it. I never asked for any of it, if you recall.'

But no, he wasn't having that. 'You did, though, little maid. Don't you remember? You asked for my help. You insisted that I marry you, and then agreed to my terms. I never forced anything on you.'

Some part of him was aware that the conversation had got out of hand somehow, and he didn't know how or why, but they were both angry and neither wanted to back down. And he suspected that it went deeper than what they were actually talking about, and that there was something they were both skirting around.

She is making you feel things again. She is making you remember what it was like to have a heart, and you do not like it.

But he didn't have a chance to think more about that because the bright little sparks in her eyes became embers, burning bright, and that was the only warning he got. Her fist came out like a shot, and she punched him squarely in the stomach.

He grunted and went back a step, muttering a curse in Greek because despite her size she was surprisingly strong and hadn't held back. He could have avoided the blow and he may well have blocked it, but he let her have the hit since part of him knew he deserved it.

'Look, I don't even know my mother, but even if I did, that's not a very nice thing to say about her,' she said accusingly, the colour in her cheeks blazing. 'You let me have that.'

He frowned, his attention caught. Had she understood the curse he'd muttered? 'Rose, do you speak Greek?'

'No,' she said. 'Why do you ask?'

'Because you understood what I said after you punched me.' And then he said it again for good measure.

A look of shock crossed her face. 'But I… I… we only spoke Russian in the compound. Where would I know Greek? How?' Her fists dropped.

'In Thailand you had a library and some of the books were in a language that looked familiar to me. I couldn't read them, though.'

Ares shoved aside his anger and the subject of Hercules and what he had and hadn't told her. 'Do you have any memories of your life before the compound?' he asked sharply. 'Any at all?'

Rose's anger had gone now too. She lifted a hand and rubbed at her temple. 'The only memory I have is of looking at some kittens in a shop.' She swallowed and then added, almost wonderingly, *'Gataki.'*

It was Greek for kitten.

A surge of an emotion Ares didn't recognise swept through him then, and he wasn't sure why it should matter to him that she must come from his own homeland, or had connections there at least, but it did.

'Perhaps you are Greek, *matia mou,*' he said softly.

Her gaze shifted to his, her big golden eyes wide with hope. 'Do you think?'

It wasn't until then that he understood how much the not knowing had affected her. She'd mentioned it a week ago, that first night beside the fire as they'd discussed a potential pregnancy, and she'd been worried about her family history. Yet that had only been the tip of the iceberg, he could see now. That hope in her eyes was desperate and he hadn't known, hadn't fully realised, just how desperate she was for her past.

That surge of emotion, inexplicable and powerful, tightened its grip, and before he even knew he was going to say it, he said like a vow, 'We will find out. I promise you, we will.'

Ares meant every word, she could see it in his gaze, hear it in his rasping stony voice. And he'd said 'we.' Not 'you' or even 'I.' It was a 'we,' as if she wasn't alone in this. As if they were going to find out together.

Her throat closed up, her anger at him and the relentless way he'd reminded her that she was the one who'd insisted on this marriage, that she hadn't had to do any of this, that the whole reason she was here and feeling all these big, complicated emotions about him was because of the choices she'd made, had drained away.

She'd shoved that unpleasant truth aside the instant he'd asked her whether she understood Greek. Because she'd understood his curse instinctively and had responded before she'd had a chance to think it through. Then the Greek word for kitten had just been sitting there in her brain, a thread of memory with it. Of kittens in a shop window and pleading with someone to let her stay there to watch them. And then a voice, a boy's, saying, 'Okay, but you have to stay right here. I won't be long.'

Greek. She might be Greek. And Ares was going to help her find out.

She tore her gaze away, her throat tight, a wave of intense emotion flooding through her so tangled she couldn't puzzle it out. Fear and hope and worry all twisted together, and the hard pinch of grief, and more she couldn't even begin to name.

Ares stepped forward and took her hands in his large, warm rough ones. 'Rose?' he said softly. 'It will be all right. We'll find out.'

She looked up at him, the hard knot of emotion pulling tight. 'What if it's terrible? What if I…have no one? What if my family is awful and I'm—'

'It will be all right,' he repeated, and it sounded like an order, as if whatever he willed, so it would be. 'We will deal with it when we get to that point, okay?'

Again, 'we' will deal with it.

Do you really want him involved with this?

She'd never expected him to help find out who she was. She'd thought she'd have to do it on her own. Except, as it turned out, now she had him. And not only his help, she understood, but his support too. Whatever she found about her family or where she came from, or anything else, it would be okay, because he would be there.

It shouldn't have made a difference and perhaps she shouldn't trust him with any of this, but…she did. She just did.

'You don't have to be part of this,' she said, giving him an out if he needed it. 'I'm sure you have other things to do.'

'I do,' he said, his hands so warm and reassuring around hers. 'But I always have other things to do. And you're my wife and this is important. So, yes, I do have to be part of this.' Amusement glinted unexpectedly in his eyes. 'Besides, I'm interested now. I want to know what kind of woman I married.'

She took a shaky breath. It was dangerous to allow him to see how afraid and yet hopeful she was about this, and maybe it would be better if she kept this part of herself hidden. Show no weakness. Don't be a victim.

He'll know. You can't hide from him.

No. He was too sharp, too perceptive, and even back in the compound, he'd seen right through her. He'd always had the ability to get under her skin. Perhaps that was why she'd asked him to help her in the first place.

Yet that was all beside the point. The real truth was that she didn't want to hide this from him. She *wanted* him to know how she felt.

Because for the first time she *didn't* have to do this alone, she had someone to help her, someone to lean on…

Ares's gaze narrowed. 'What is it? There's something else you're worried about. I can see it in your eyes.'

She swallowed and looked at him squarely. 'What if the problem isn't them? What if the problem is me? What if I find out who my family is and they…?' The words stuck in her throat, that most secret fear hard to get out. But she forced herself to continue. 'What if we contact them and they…they don't want me? What if they don't want to know?'

His expression didn't change as per usual, but something in his silver-green eyes flared. 'Why would you think that?'

She couldn't look at him all of a sudden. She didn't want him to see the fear that gripped her. The terrible fear that had haunted her at nights sometimes when she couldn't sleep. When loneliness had set in and her future stretched out before her, a future that contained nothing but basic survival, years of being told what to do and cleaning rooms and being treated like dirt. Years of being trapped in the same place and never being able to leave, never being able to see the outside world. No hope. No dreams. Just endless loneliness.

The fear that no one would come for her, because no one had wanted her. She'd been abducted and trafficked, and her family had simply let her go. Intellectually she knew that might not be the case, that maybe her family had been searching for her all this time, but... how would she know? And, more importantly, when the time came to find out the truth, did she want to know it?

She stared down at his large, scarred hands and her own engulfed in them. His touch was warm, the strength in those hands reassuring. Strength enough to keep her safe and hold her together, warmth enough to chase away the cold loneliness that curled inside her even now.

'No one came for me, Ares,' she said, her voice gone nearly as raspy as his. 'And I know, perhaps they just couldn't find me. The traffickers hid their tracks well. But still, no one came. Some nights I used to wonder why that was, why I was just left there in the compound to rot.' She swallowed hard against the sudden lump in her throat. 'And I wonder sometimes if I'd done something wrong and this was a punishment. That I didn't deserve to be rescued.'

There was a moment of silence and in it she heard her own stupid, ridiculous voice, all hoarse with fear and pain. A victim's voice.

He must think her so pathetic. He was a

warrior and he valued strength, and she wasn't being strong. She was being broken.

Rose jerked her hands from his abruptly and turned to go, unable to even be in the same room as him while she felt so small and weak. Yet she only took two steps before iron fingers wrapped around her upper arm and she found herself pulled up against his big, hard body.

Her back was to his chest, his heat burning through her sports bra and yoga pants as if they weren't even there. She strained at little against his grip, but then his other hand gripped her other arm, and she was held fast.

Her heartbeat thundered and there were tears in her eyes. She didn't want him to let her go, but she couldn't bear him to see her vulnerability. She thought she was fine with it, but she wasn't. It felt too raw and too painful.

But his grip only tightened, keeping her right where she was.

Then his mouth was near her ear, his warm breath on her skin, making her whole body burn with that desire, a heat that was always smouldering, ready to burst into flames at any moment.

'Listen to me,' he murmured. 'You were a child. You did not deserve to be abducted from the street and sold to the highest bidder. No child deserves that. No *person* deserves that. *None* of what happened to you was your fault.'

Rose closed her eyes, feeling tears start in them, which was silly. She didn't know why she was crying. She didn't know why what he said hurt, because it did hurt. 'Then why did it happen?' She sounded like a wounded bird, desperate and afraid, and she hated it, yet she couldn't seem to keep herself from speaking. 'Why did it happen to me?'

'Because it did.' His voice was harsh, a note of ferocity in it. 'Because sometimes bad things happen to people who do not deserve them. That's life. But that's not the end of the story, Rose, and that's *not* the end of yours. It's what you do after that matters. That's the only thing that matters. You endured and you survived, and you got out, and you did that all on your own.'

'No, I had you—'

'But you had to ask me first. You had to find the courage to ask a man you'd never met, a man with the most terrible scars, for help in a place where no one was your friend. Where even saying the words could get you a terrible punishment. And you found that courage, little maid. You took it in both hands, and you looked me in the eye, and you asked me.' His fingers tightened on her upper arms, just on the edge of pain. 'That's why I called you a warrior. Because it was a warrior I saw that day. Not a victim. Not a servant. Not a girl someone left behind, a person that no one wanted. A woman who knew her own worth and refused to play the hand life had dealt her. A woman who was going to play her own game, with her own rules.'

There was no hesitation in his voice. Only certainty. As if he was stating facts and nothing more, and it made her throat ache, made tears slide gently down her face.

'I don't want you to think that I'm weak,' she said hoarsely. 'I don't want you to think I'm a victim. You're so strong and I—'

'And you are too. I told you that.' Then, shockingly, his teeth closed around one of the cords of her neck, the gentle bite sending a shock wave of sensation through her. 'So why don't you show me? Show me how strong you are, little maid. Right here, right now.'

And he bit her again.

Rose shuddered, the heat already beginning to build inside her, and that was better than this other feeling, this intense, powerful, dizzying feeling that was coiling in her heart. That had felt every single word he'd said and had carved them into her soul. So she wouldn't forget. Because if he saw that in her, then it must be true.

She *was* that warrior. And maybe it was time for her to own it.

Except Ares let her go, the heat of his body at her back vanishing, and she spun round in surprise.

He'd taken a couple of steps back and was staring at her challengingly. Then he arched a brow. So, she came at him, one fist flying out. His fingers closed around her wrist yet again, but this time he pulled her into him, his other hand grabbing her ponytail and holding onto it as he took her mouth like the conqueror he was.

He was not holding back, she knew that immediately. Also, that he was expecting her to give as good as she got, so she did, kissing him back as if she owned him, as if he was hers and always had been.

Her teeth sunk into his bottom lip, and she bit him hard. He made a growling sound deep in his chest and then they were down on the mat, her on her back with him on top of her, a heavy weight pressing her down.

She loved the feeling, loved how he surrounded her and anchored her, making her feel safe and protected. Yet today she didn't need anchoring or protecting, today she wanted to be his match in every way, so she growled at him and shoved, and then they were turning over, with her on top and held astride him.

He sat up, pulling off her black sports bra with ease, while she clawed at the black T-shirt he wore. Then she pushed him onto his back again, her hands going to the athletic shorts he wore, trying to pull them down. He murmured a curse, and they were rolling over once more, him on top, his hands firm and strong as he tugged down her yoga pants and underwear.

She panted, writhing naked beneath him, his hands stroking and pinching and caressing, while she bit his shoulder and pulled at the waistband of his shorts. There was another curse and they rolled yet again, him on his back, her above, and the rest of his clothing gone. He was naked as she was, and her hands found the long, thick length of him. He was smooth and velvety and iron hard, and when she stroked him, he cursed yet again. She wanted to drive him as insane as he drove her, except she had no patience for that, not today. Instead, she gripped him and shifted her hips, letting him push inside her, the long, sweet slide of him making her shudder and shake.

Then his hands settled like brands on her skin, gripping her tight, showing her how to move with him, how to ride him to bring them both the greatest pleasure.

It was intoxicating, heady, to be astride this powerful man, to brace herself on his broad scarred chest, watch the flex and release of all those hard, carved muscles. Erotic too, to know that those muscles honed by violence could yet bring her the most intense pleasure.

His eyes were bright silver as they stared up at her, his face tense with hunger. The push and pull of him inside her was too much, too intense, and yet not enough.

'Ares,' she groaned, shaking. 'More.'

Again, they rolled, and then she was being pressed down hard into the mat as he lifted her legs up and around his waist, driving himself inside her, over and over again until the whole world was fire.

And she was exploding, melting, coming apart.

Until she was nothing but sparks drifting slowly in the air.

For a moment they lay like that together as they both caught their breath, and then Ares rolled them one last time, onto their sides, with her caught fast in his arms and held against his powerful body. Then he pressed a kiss into her hair. 'We can start searching for where you came from today,' he said. 'We don't have to wait.'

But Rose's chest clenched tight. It was good lying in his arms. Good just being with him and she wanted to enjoy it. They only had another week, and she didn't want to think about anything else.

'Can we do it later?' she asked him. 'I want to have this last week with only you.'

He said nothing, and when she glanced up at him, she met his gaze looking back. Something she couldn't name glinted in his eyes. 'You don't have to be afraid, Rose. I told you it would be all right and it will be.'

'I know. I just...don't want to think about that right now. We only have a week left and I'd rather spend it doing this.' And she lifted her hips for emphasis.

His mouth curved in one of his rare, precious warm smiles that made her heart flutter behind her ribs. 'In that case, it can wait. I am all yours.'

And for the whole of the next week, that's exactly what he was.

CHAPTER EIGHT

Winter

ARES STOOD ON the frozen lake that served as a helipad for the lakefront lodge in Iceland that he liked to retreat to during winter and watched as the helicopter bringing Rose from the airport touched down.

It was a still, clear night, the stars glittering in the black sky above like hard chips of diamond, the temperature well below freezing. Behind him was the lodge, all lit up and warmly welcoming so she wouldn't have to bear the freezing temperatures for too long. He'd hurry her inside, let her get settled and then he'd tell her what he'd found.

Her identity.

His staff had only brought him actual confirmation right before his jet had left the States where he'd been completing some business, so he hadn't had long to contemplate it. But it was good news and he wanted to be the one to bring it to her.

Since leaving the Cotswolds he'd put an entire department of his best people onto finding out Rose's identity. They didn't have much to go on—her general age and the possibility that she was Greek—but it was enough to start a search and he did have a lot of resources at his disposal.

His team had trawled police reports and found evidence of many missing girls in Greece around the time that Rose could potentially have been abducted, and one by one they'd dismissed them, apart from a couple.

Yet Ares knew there was only one possibility from that list: Ismena Xenakis, abducted as a child from the streets of Athens twenty years earlier.

The report had been filed by her older brother, Castor Xenakis, but nothing had ever been investigated.

Ares knew of a Castor Xenakis. He'd once been a notorious playboy known for his various shady criminal underworld connections who'd suddenly cleaned up his act, married a woman who'd once been a supermarket checkout girl—if the press could be believed—and was now a respectable family man.

It had to be the same Castor Xenakis who'd lost his sister. The name was too unusual. Further investigations had also revealed that Castor Xenakis had led a secret life infiltrating trafficking rings and passing the information on to relevant authorities, which virtually guaranteed him to be the same man.

Ares had debated contacting him, but then dismissed the idea. It wasn't his place. He had to bring the information to Rose first before anything else, because the conversation they'd had in the gym at the manor house had stuck in his head, as had the fear in her beautiful golden eyes. The fear that no one had looked for her because no one had wanted her. Even now the memory of the pain in her voice made his own chest tighten, though he didn't want to think about why that was.

What he was clear about was that she had to know she wasn't alone. That she had an older brother, and that if he was the kind of man he was reputed to be, he hadn't stopped looking for her. That he'd been looking for her for the past twenty years.

The rotors slowed and Ares ducked beneath them, walking over to pull open the helicopter door. And felt something akin to an electric shock as he met Rose's bright gaze. She smiled, her lovely face lighting up at the sight of him, and that strange feeling in his chest, the one that had tightened in response to her pain, now tightened again in response to that smile.

You are getting emotionally involved with her.

No, he wasn't. He was pleased to see her because he liked her and felt empathetic towards her, but that was all. Certainly nothing more.

She was all wrapped up in the thick pale blue parka he'd had sent to her, a scarf and hat to match, plus gloves. She looked so beautiful he could barely hold himself back from reaching for her.

But then she flung off her headset and launched herself into his arms and her mouth was on his, making it very clear that she'd missed him.

You missed her too.

He tightened his arms around her and kissed her back hard. Yes, he had missed her. In his bed. Fifteen years of celibacy had never bothered him, yet the past three months without her had been agony. He'd been counting down the days until winter, until it was time for their two weeks, and once he'd told her about her brother, he was going to take her to bed and keep her there for days. Maybe even a whole week. After all, it was winter in Iceland and there wasn't much else to do.

The lodge staff were already hauling out her luggage, so Ares lifted her from the helicopter himself, carrying her in his arms across the frozen lake, the chilly air bringing a flush to her cheeks.

'You don't need to carry me,' she protested, not making any attempt to dislodge herself from his grip. 'I can walk.'

'Very well.' He stopped, making a show of letting her down.

She laughed and wrapped her arms around his neck, snuggling into him. 'On second thoughts, it's too cold to walk.'

He grinned and resumed striding towards the lodge, feeling as if a weight had been pressing down on him and now that she was here it was gone. It made him feel ridiculously light.

She nestled against him, turning her face against the thick down jacket he'd pulled on to meet her, and they were both silent as he stepped from the ice to the small wooden jetty that projected into the lake, then went up some stone steps that led up to the lodge itself.

A large wooden deck fronted the lake, with big, sliding glass doors that led into the lodge's main living area. One of his staff pulled open the door for them and he stepped through into the warmth of the living area, the door pushed shut behind him.

He didn't want to let her go. He wanted to head straight up the stairs to the comfortable bedroom and big wooden bed and do all the things he'd been fantasising about for the past three months. But this news couldn't wait.

He let her down and then stepped back as the staff member who'd handled the door discreetly withdrew.

She pulled off her hat as the warmth of the room penetrated, her cheeks flushed and her golden eyes glittering. 'Were you disappointed?' she asked suddenly.

He didn't pretend he didn't know what she meant. 'That you weren't pregnant? No.'

She'd sent him an email a month after their time in the Cotswolds, letting him know that she hadn't ended up being pregnant. He'd told himself it was fine, that if she chose to stay with him, they'd have plenty of time to try for children, then had shoved all thoughts of pregnancy and the fact that this was the last two weeks he'd have with her before she made her choice out of his head.

They had more important things to discuss now.

'Are you sure?' she asked. 'I know you wanted—'

'The pregnancy conversation can wait, Rose,' he interrupted, impatient. 'I have something to tell you.'

She looked like she might say something

more, but then clearly thinking better of it, merely raised an eyebrow. 'Oh?'

'I've found out who you are.'

Her face went white. 'What?'

He'd known it would be a shock, so he took a step forward, putting his hands on her hips to steady her. 'I know your real name, Rose.'

She stared up at him, golden eyes wide, as if she'd never seen him before her life.

'Your name is—'

She laid her fingers across his lips, silencing him. Her face was still pale, all the light and happiness she'd shown him in the helicopter gone as if it had never been, her fingertips a gentle pressure.

You fool. Did you really have to spring it on her like that? Especially given her reluctance to talk about it over the past three months.

He'd broached the topic several times in various emails about the search for her identity, letting her know that he had considerable resources and he could help if she wanted him to. She'd replied that yes, if he could help, that would be appreciated, but it was clear she hadn't expected him to discover the truth.

She took her hand from his mouth, then stepped away, moving over to the big open fire that stood at one end of the room. The flames burned brightly, firelight dancing over her pale face, reminding him of that night in the Cotswolds where he'd taken her in front of the fire there.

His body hardened, aware that it had been three months without her, and it was hungry for her.

He ignored it. Now was not the time.

'It's good news, Rose,' he said quietly. 'I think you'd like to hear it.'

There was another silence.

'So, you get to know everything about me, but I know nothing about you.' She unzipped her parka, staring down at the flames.

Ares frowned. 'You know about me. I told you—'

'You told me about you being in the Legion and that you'd lost your wife. That's it.' She pulled off her gloves, throwing them with a sudden, forceful movement onto the nearby couch. 'You know my real name, but I don't even know how you got burned.'

A whisper of the guilt and defensive anger he'd felt during their discussion in the gym, about his company, threaded through him once again. Guilt that he hadn't told her anything about himself and anger because he didn't want to.

Everything was so tangled up with Naya and he didn't discuss her with anyone.

Anyway, he was here with the truth of who she was, and he didn't understand why she didn't want to hear it, or why she was making this about him.

'This isn't about me,' he said. 'This is about you. Don't you want to know?'

She didn't turn, pulling off her hat and throwing it on the couch along with the gloves, a wealth of golden hair tumbling out. It was much longer now, to her waist.

'I don't like that you know more about me than I do about you,' she said, ignoring his question. 'You always did. Why is your past off limits and yet you feel free to pry into every aspect of mine?'

Ares gritted his teeth, his anger gaining a dull edge of disappointment. He'd thought she'd be happy about this. 'You told me you were fine with me helping you discover your origins. I asked you and you said yes.'

'I was fine with it.' She turned her head and glanced at him, her gaze brilliant with temper. 'But I didn't think you'd be the one to discover it first. And I didn't think that you'd have everything of me, while I had nothing of you.'

She's right. You have *given her nothing.*

Yes, but giving her something of himself assumed a relationship that they didn't have. A relationship that they would never have either.

You want it, though.

He ignored that.

'I told you back in England that my past is irrelevant,' he said curtly.

'Oh, and mine isn't?' Sparks glittered like embers from a wildfire in her eyes. 'Why do you get to hold onto your secrets? And anyway, it *is* relevant. The fact that you were married is relevant. The fact that half your body is scar tissue is relevant. What kind of marriage are we going to have if you can't even talk to me about it?'

She'd said it as if staying married to him was a foregone conclusion and not a choice she had yet to make, and it made something inside him lurch like he'd missed a step going up a staircase.

He'd thought he wouldn't care if she chose to stay married to him or not. But he did care. He cared very much, and he shouldn't.

'But that is not a foregone conclusion, is it, Rose?' he bit out. 'The year is not yet up. You might not choose to stay married to me.'

Her cheeks were already pink, but he didn't miss how they went a little pinker, as if she'd made a slip she hadn't meant to. 'It's true, I might not,' she agreed. 'But you could give me a reason to stay.'

'I didn't realise that mattered to you,' he said roughly.

'What? Getting to know each other?' One blond brow rose imperiously. 'Not initially, no. But then you went on and on about how important it was that we got comfortable with each other, how I had to learn what being a wife meant, and blah, blah, blah. So I changed my mind. And yes, it does matter to me. You made it matter with your big song and dance.'

She was angry. He stared at her, trying to see what the real issue was. 'Rose—'

'Tell me, Ares,' she said flatly. 'Tell me what happened to you.'

That is *the real issue. You know everything about her, and she knows nothing about you, and that isn't fair. And besides, since when did it become a big secret?*

It wasn't a big secret. It had never been before, even though he didn't talk about it with anyone, so why was he so reluctant? Yes, she'd probably blame him the way he blamed himself, but what of it? He wasn't supposed to care about anyone's opinion anyway, let alone hers.

It was a small thing to give her, and after all, it was an old grief. He could just tell her and be done, and then the subject would be behind them. She wouldn't ask again.

'Fine,' he said harshly. 'What happened to me?

The village I grew up in was full of factions and old feuds. People fighting each other. One of the more powerful groups started demanding protection money from people, but I refused to pay. Naya and I hadn't been married long and I was…very proud. The Aristiades name meant strength and I didn't want to look weak or cowardly in front of her. I thought I could protect her, but… They came in the night, with petrol bombs. Our house went up in flames.' He couldn't remember much about the actual fire, the only mercy he'd been given. 'I had been out with my father, helping him with some livestock, and when I got home the whole place was alight. I went in to rescue Naya, but the flames were too fierce. A beam fell on me, and my father had to drag me out. I spent a couple of years recovering from the burns.'

You failed her. It was your fault.

Oh, he knew that. He knew that all too well. The pain from his burns had faded, but the guilt in his heart never had. It was his punishment to always feel it.

Rose was staring at him, her eyes wide, a terrible sympathy glittering in them.

He had to force the words out, but he managed it. 'Naya died because of me.'

The fire was warm at Rose's back, the heat of the lodge's living room warming her through.

Yet it felt as if she'd plunged through the ice of the frozen lake outside and into the water beneath it.

Cold shock swept through her, the fire making no difference to the chill that found its way deep into her bones.

He'd lost his wife in a terrible way and somehow blamed himself for it.

He stood not far from her, dressed for the cold in a thick black parka, and the expression on his face was so hard he may as well have been carved from the granite of the mountains surrounding the lodge. There was no deep green in his gaze now, or sparks of glittering silver. They looked dark as the night outside.

And she was conscious of a tearing grief inside her, for him and what he'd lost, and it was all she could do to shove it aside, but she managed it. This wasn't about her pain, this was about his.

You should never have forced this from him.

She swallowed past the lump in her throat. She'd known pushing him to tell her his secrets wasn't fair, that it wouldn't be a pleasant story, but she'd never dreamed it would be so awful.

Tears prickled behind her eyes, and she had to look away, blinking fiercely. She didn't know what to say, everything seemed so inadequate, even an apology.

Still, she gave it to him anyway. 'I'm sorry,' she said huskily, all the anger and fear that had filled her when he'd told her he knew who she was draining away. 'I didn't know.'

'Of course you didn't know.' His voice was even more raspy than it normally was. 'I didn't tell you.'

'I'm sorry,' she said again, uselessly. 'I only wanted—'

'She went to sleep and never woke up,' Ares interrupted as if she hadn't spoken. 'That's what they told me. Smoke inhalation.' He sounded as icy as the lake outside, as if the terrible facts didn't touch him. 'It was years ago. I have moved past it now.'

Her breath shuddered in and out, the pain sitting just behind her ribs an ache she didn't know what to do with. She blinked her tears back fiercely and forced her gaze back to his, because it was cowardly to look away, to not even be brave enough to witness his pain.

And no matter what he'd said about moving past it, she could still hear that pain. His voice might be cold and his expression hard and set, but she could hear agony in the roughened, frayed timbre of his voice. She could see it in the darkness of his eyes. His physical wounds had healed, leaving him with terrible scars, but this hurt went soul-deep. And it had scarred him inside just as deeply as he'd been scarred on the outside.

She wanted to put her arms around him, comfort him, but he was radiating tension and she knew instinctively he wouldn't welcome it. So, she pushed her hands into the pockets of her parka, and said, 'You…shouldn't blame yourself, Ares.'

'Should I not?' Each word sounded as if it had been carved from ice. 'What I should have done was pay them. But I was too proud. I did not want to look like a coward.'

'But you weren't the one with the petrol bombs—'

'No,' he said flatly, a muscle flicking in his hard jaw, the light making jagged shadows with his scars. 'No, we will not talk about this. I want to tell you what I found out about you.'

Her heart ached, fear seeping through her again.

This wasn't how she'd wanted her final two weeks with him to go. She'd wanted it to be like it had been in England, in his bed, in his arms. Spending time with him, learning how to defend herself, or watching all the movies she'd missed out on. Rambling in the woods. Lying in the huge claw-foot bath that was big enough to accommodate both of them, while his hands roamed lazily over her, relating new things she'd found out or discussing the latest scientific advances, which she'd discovered quite an interest in. She'd loved those days. She'd loved talking to him. He was fiercely intelligent and quick, and sometimes she argued with him purely because she loved doing that too.

She'd been looking forward to seeing him so much that the past three months had felt like they'd dragged. She hadn't been able to stop thinking about him. She'd even been surprisingly disappointed when her period had arrived, though she wasn't sure why when she hadn't wanted to be pregnant.

She'd wanted to discuss that now too, and not think about the wild leap of her heart the moment the helicopter door had opened, and his silver-green eyes had met hers. Or the pure joy that had filled her as he'd pulled her out of the helicopter and carried her over the ice, the frigid wind biting at her nose.

Those things she could examine later, but in this moment, it was the thrill of his presence that she'd wanted. And then he'd told her he'd discovered who she was and all of that had disappeared in a flood of cold shock, followed by an irrational anger.

That she knew her anger was defensive didn't help, because she also knew what lay underneath it: fear. Now the moment of truth was here, and she'd been a coward. And she'd turned that fear back on him. It wasn't fair of her. It wasn't right.

She'd spoiled things.

Her hands clenched tight in the pockets of her parka, and she wanted to apologise for that as well, but that was all about her own insecurities and the time wasn't right for them now, so she ignored the apologies sitting on her tongue. Ignored the flicker of selfish hurt that he didn't want to share his grief with her, even though she knew she had no right to it.

Instead, she braced herself and said, 'Okay. Tell me then.'

'Your name is Ismena Xenakis and you were born in Athens. Your mother appears to be dead, your father unknown. But you have an older brother. His name is Castor Xenakis. He's CEO of CX Enterprises, a multi-billion-dollar company dealing in all kinds of different industries. He is married and has one child.'

'Okay, Izzy. You can look at the kittens,' he'd said, already turning away to the shop next door. 'But you have to stay right here while I get the ice creams. Don't move. I won't be long...'

The kittens had been so cute, and she'd done as she was told, staying right where Cas had said. But then she'd seen another kitten across the street, so small and lost-looking. Cas had been gone a long time, and she'd got tired of waiting. The kitten had needed someone to look after it, and so she'd crossed the street and...

Her heartbeat thudded hard in her head, her skull aching. There was bile at the back of her throat.

She'd bent to pick up the kitten and someone had grabbed her from behind. She'd been so shocked she hadn't made a sound. A bag had been put over her head and she'd been bundled under someone's arm only to be tossed onto something hard. Then a door had slammed shut and she'd felt movement. It had been only then that she'd screamed.

By then it had been too late... It had been far, far too late.

Rose took a breath and then another, and then Ares's hand was at her hip, guiding her to sit on the long, low, black leather sofa.

Her brother. Castor. She couldn't remember his face, couldn't remember anything about him except a feeling of safety and warmth whenever he was near. And his voice, newly deepening into a man's, telling her to stay put.

But you didn't, did you?

She shut her eyes against painful tears, swallowing the sob in her throat.

'He has spent the past twenty years looking for you,' Ares went on relentlessly. 'I had several contacts confirm that he was involved in infiltrating trafficking rings and passing information on to the authorities, and I can only assume he was doing that in order to find you. I also have it on good authority that now he uses his many private residences as safe houses for women with nowhere to go and no one to turn to.'

She swallowed again, but that sob wouldn't go away.

Ares didn't touch her, but she wanted him to. She wanted his strong arms around her, to turn her face into his chest, press herself against all his reassuring heat. Because she felt weak and needed his strength.

But he wasn't touching her, and she knew it was because of what she'd said to him. Because of the confession she'd forced from him when he hadn't been ready for it, uncovering a grief that went too deep.

So, who was she to cry over the discovery of her true name and a brother she'd forgotten? A brother who'd never stopped looking for even after all these years. Who was she to be upset about finding a family, when he'd lost his wife so terribly? A loss he blamed himself for.

Forcing down the sobs and fiercely blinking back her tears, she lifted her head. Ares was standing next to the couch, his hands in the pockets of his jeans. His face wore its customary granite expression, but anger glittered in his eyes. And, well, he had a right to it, didn't he?

He wasn't there to reassure her, not that she deserved it anyway. Not after what she'd made him confess.

'Th-thank you,' she forced out. 'For finding all that out for me. I appreciate it.'

The hard expression on his face didn't change. 'Do you? Didn't seem like you were all that grateful just before.'

'I… I know. I was just…afraid.' Her jaw ached with the effort of holding back the sobs. 'But I'm fine now and, really, I am grateful, Ares. It's just…a lot.' She pushed herself to her feet, needing suddenly to be alone so she could weep in private. She didn't want to put her grief and fear and apprehension about what he'd just told her onto him. 'I need…to go and freshen up. Is my room up the stairs? You don't have to show me, I can find it myself.'

That muscle in his jaw leapt again. 'There is only one bedroom in the main house. We are sharing it.'

Her stomach tightened. So he'd expected that she would be sleeping with him. Ten minutes earlier she'd have been ecstatic. Now all she wanted was some space.

'Okay,' she said thickly. 'That's fine. Is it up-stairs?'

He nodded and gestured towards the stairs. He didn't offer to show her where it was. Apparently, they both needed space.

A set of wooden stairs led up to the upper level of the lodge, where there was a huge bedroom and an equally huge bathroom. Her luggage had been put at the foot of the giant four-poster bed in the bedroom. The bed faced windows that looked out over the lake. It had a smooth, rustic wooden floor covered with rugs and plain white walls, the bed with its giant posts and white linen hangings the centrepiece of the room.

She sat on the edge of it and allowed herself a few moments to weep, her emotions so tangled and twisted she didn't even know why she was crying.

Her name was Ismena Xenakis and she had a brother. A brother who'd been looking for her all this time.

She hadn't been forgotten. And she wasn't alone.

Ares found this for you. He discovered it.

Tears slid slowly down her cheeks, and she didn't bother to wipe them away. Her chest ached with grief and fear and hope and guilt. Grief for the years lost and fear that her brother wouldn't want to see her. Hope that he would, and she would find him again. Guilt for not doing what he'd said on that street so long ago. Guilt for not staying and watching those kittens, because perhaps if she'd done what she'd been told, she wouldn't have been taken.

And beneath all of that lay a deeper ache. For Ares and what he'd told her and where that left them.

Why does he matter so much? You're married to him, but you're not really his wife, are you? You forced him to marry you. He would never have chosen you.

All of that was true, and she didn't know why he'd come to matter to her so much. It was only that he'd been kind to her. No, not just kind; he'd made her feel like she was more than an abducted girl sold to be a servant in a rich man's house. A powerless victim of human trafficking. He'd given her freedom and helped her make a life for herself, and over the past few months as she'd worked at the cafe, little daydreams of having a family of her own, a family with him, had danced in her head.

She hadn't realised she'd even wanted that until she'd discovered she wasn't pregnant, after all. And had been so oddly disappointed.

Nine months ago, in Thailand, she'd thought

she'd never want to stay being his wife. Now… it was different.

It's different because of him. Because you're falling for him.

No, of course she wasn't falling for him. That would be stupid in the extreme, and anyway, she'd never fallen for anyone before so how would she even know if she had?

And apart from all of that, he'd be the worst person to fall for since it was clear he was still grieving his first wife. He might say he'd moved on, but a man of such intense passions didn't move on so easily.

Rose scrubbed her tears away. There was no point in thinking about her feelings for Ares, no matter what they were. She wasn't even sure she was going to choose to stay married to him, and even if she did, she didn't know if he'd want that too. Because it was his choice as well, not just hers.

Regardless, she needed to stop thinking about her feelings and concentrate on the most immediate issue, which was the fact that she now had an identity. She could contact her brother to let him know she was alive.

Except, before that, if she wanted to have the two weeks she'd initially planned, she was going to have to make things right with Ares. She'd apologised for how she'd pushed him, and then she'd thanked him for finding Castor. She couldn't keep on doing both so perhaps the best way forward was to put the tension of what had happened just before aside and carry on as if it hadn't happened.

She wouldn't mention his wife again. She'd leave it up to him if he wanted to talk about it. Then with any luck they could go back to what they'd had in the Cotswolds, that warm intimacy, along with all the physical affection too.

In fact, maybe she should have a shower, then put on the pretty dress she'd spent some of her savings on, the one the sales assistant had assured her would drive her husband mad with desire. Then she'd show him exactly how much she'd missed him.

Pushing herself off the bed, Rose scrubbed away the last of her tears, then strode decisively into the bathroom and turned on the shower.

CHAPTER NINE

ARES STOOD IN front of the fire and knocked back the rest of the very good vodka he'd poured himself, hoping the icy burn of the alcohol would cool the anger that coiled like a dragon inside him.

He'd been petty with Rose, and he knew it. He'd let his anger get the better of him, and that was not permitted. Another example of him not learning the lessons the past had taught him.

He didn't know how she'd got beneath his defences, but she had, and it was clear to him that he had to stop her from getting any further beneath them. Somehow.

So what if the sympathy in her face and the glitter of grief in her eyes had tugged at something painful inside him even though he hadn't wanted it to? So what if she'd told him that he didn't need to blame himself? She was wrong. She was just wrong.

And he wasn't supposed to care. Yet he'd been

angry at having to tell her about Naya, and that anger, both at her and with himself, had made him petty, refusing to comfort her distress as he'd told her about her brother. He hadn't even put his arms around her.

You didn't have to tell her about Naya. That was your choice. It's not fair to take it out on her.

Ares put his empty tumbler on the mantelpiece and stared down into the flames.

It was true, he couldn't say she'd forced him. He'd made the decision to tell her, and it was his own misjudgement that he'd kept it a secret in the first place. Turning it all into a big deal. That was hardly Rose's fault.

He let out a breath, rubbing at his brow. He should apologise, especially if he wanted these next two weeks to be as blissful as the last couple in the Cotswolds had been. She'd been distressed and him not doing anything to ease her or comfort her had been cruel, and yes, very petty.

Ares turned from the fire, intending on going upstairs to find her, then froze.

Rose was standing in the doorway. She wore a crimson silk dress with a deep vee neckline and little straps, cut on the bias to hug every one of her generous curves. The colour made her golden skin glow and brought out the sparks in her eyes, her hair a golden halo around her head.

She looked stunningly beautiful.

His body hardened instantly, the weight of the past three months of celibacy descending on him like an anvil. All he wanted was to stride over to her, shove her against a wall and rip her dress away, pour all this sullen anger into her until ecstasy carried it all away.

But he stayed where he was, tense with the effort of mastering himself, because he had an apology to make.

She gave him an uncertain smile. 'Do you like my dress? I wasn't sure about it, but the saleswoman said my husband would love it.'

Her husband. Him.

It hit him hard right then. He'd had no issues with thinking about her as his wife, but for some reason, thinking of himself as her husband hadn't occurred to him. But he was.

And will you fail her like you failed Naya?

A shiver of an emotion he couldn't identify went through him, chilling him.

He ignored it. 'Your dress is beautiful,' he murmured, letting her see the appreciation in his eyes. 'And so are you.'

She flushed, looking pleased. 'Thank you.'

'I hope you let me pay for that.'

'No.' A little spark glittered in her eyes, a hint

of challenge that went straight to his groin. 'I used my own money.'

Part of him wanted to argue with her about it, challenge her the way she challenged him, and then finish their argument in the way they both loved so much: in bed.

But that could wait.

He held her gaze. 'I owe you an apology, Rose.'

Her eyes widened. 'Oh?'

For a second, he wondered if she'd even picked up on his anger earlier. She hadn't reached for him when he'd told her the name of her brother, after all. She hadn't even looked at him, keeping her attention squarely on her hands.

But even if she hadn't realised, he still wanted her to know he was sorry for it.

'You were upset,' he said. 'And I didn't help.'

Her long, thick golden lashes lowered, veiling her gaze. 'It's fine.'

'It isn't fine. I should have been there for you, and I wasn't, because I was angry. It was petty and unfair of me.' The words were surprisingly easy to say.

'It wasn't unfair.' She smoothed her dress. 'I shouldn't have pushed you about...' She stopped, her hands still moving nervously on the fabric.

She was upset, he could hear it in her voice, and before he knew what he was doing, he'd closed the distance between them, going to where she stood in the doorway and reaching for her. His hands found her hips, the fabric of her dress warm against his skin, and he tugged her close. She didn't resist, her nervous fingers resting at last on his chest, and she looked up at him, something that looked like guilt in her eyes.

'I'm sorry,' she said before he could speak. 'I shouldn't have made you talk about your wife. I didn't mean to hurt you. I just wanted to know you better and I shouldn't have pushed.'

'Again, you didn't know.' He tightened his hands on her hips, the warmth of her seeping into him, familiar and yet new, making him want to do so many different things to her. Things he'd been dreaming about since those two weeks in the Cotswolds. 'And you were right to push. It's not a secret and it's not fair of me to keep it like one. Besides, you didn't force me. I chose to tell you in the end.'

Her big golden eyes were full of sympathy and a compassion that made his heart ache for reasons he couldn't have articulated. Especially when neither sympathy nor compassion was what he wanted.

Not when you don't deserve it.

Ah, but he knew that. He'd always known that.

'You don't have to tell me anything more,' she said with quiet finality. 'I'll never mention it again.'

It was what he wanted. His wife existing only in his memory, in his conscience, in the company he'd built to honour her, the only evidence of his failure the scars on his face. After all, he wasn't going to make those same mistakes again.

He'd allowed his pride and his anger to talk him into thinking he was strong enough to protect the woman he loved, and he hadn't thought through the consequences.

His emotions had blinded him; he couldn't trust them to guide him properly, only the memory of his wife could do that.

Sex, though, that was only physical, and he could allow himself that.

He bent his head and kissed her upturned mouth, let the sweet taste of her fill his senses as he explored her. She gave the most delicious shiver and melted against him, her pliant body pressed the length of his. He adjusted her hips, settling the heat between her thighs against the growing hardness of his groin, and he heard her give a little moan.

He dropped one hand from her hip, finding the hem of her dress and sliding his palm beneath it to the silky skin of her thigh. She felt so warm and her mouth beneath his was so hot.

But what about her? What about what she deserves?

The strange chill that had crept through him before did so again, deepening this time, so that even through the heat of their kiss and the warmth of her skin, he felt it.

She deserved all the things she'd never had, all the things that had been denied her as a prisoner. And if she chose to stay, he would give them to her. Freedom to go anywhere, do anything. Money to buy whatever she wanted or donate to charity if she preferred. Passion to keep her hunger satisfied and support to help her branch out into whichever career she wanted to satisfy her intellect.

That's not all she deserves.

His heartbeat was far too loud and the chill creeping through him was getting wider and deeper. He kissed her harder, pushing her up against the wall and pressing himself against her, wanting her heat to chase it away.

She was rocking against him, trying to ease her own need, her fingers curled in his shirt. Kissing him back so hungrily and so desperately.

Yet all the hunger and the desperation in the world wasn't a match for the ice that wrapped itself around his heart, and before he knew what he was doing, he'd pushed himself away from her.

Her eyes were wide, her cheeks flushed with the effects of their kiss. She blinked. 'Ares? What's wrong?'

He took a breath, fighting his growing sense of disquiet.

That all the things he wanted to give her wouldn't ever be enough. That she should have more than that, that she *deserved* more than that.

She deserves to be treated as a true wife should. With love.

He turned away from her suddenly, striding back to fire and grabbing the tumbler off the mantelpiece. He went over to the drinks cabinet where the vodka bottle sat and opened it, splashing some more into the glass.

'Ares?' Rose's voice was full of uncertainty.

He took a swallow of the vodka and glanced over to where she stood. She looked half ravaged; her pretty mouth was full and red from his kiss, a flush creeping down her golden skin and under the creased silk of her dress.

Theos, how he wanted her. Had he wanted Naya this badly? He couldn't remember.

You know it's true. You know that's what you should give her.

He didn't want to acknowledge it, not any part of it, but it crept through his brain all the same. Somehow, at some point in this past year, the heart he'd thought had died with Naya had started beating again, and Rose was the one who'd restarted it.

And now she mattered to him, which was not what he'd wanted or planned for.

His heart was supposed to stay dead along with his wife.

But he could feel the pull inside him towards her, the need to cross the distance between them once again, to have the pleasure of her silken skin beneath his hands, and the hot clasp of her sex around his. Her breath in his ear and her touch on his body. And it wasn't just physical, because if it had been, any woman would have satisfied him right then.

But he didn't want just any woman.

He wanted her and her alone. And he had from the first moment he'd met her.

But why should you be allowed to have her? You had a woman once before, remember? And you killed her. You do not deserve a second chance.

'Ares?' Rose was closer now, the firelight gilding her gorgeous figure. 'What's the matter? Did I do something I shouldn't?'

'No,' he said roughly. 'Tell me, what are you going to do about your brother?'

The change of subject was so sudden Rose just stared at him. She was still trembling from the effects of that kiss, her mouth hot and sensitive, the place on her thigh where he'd touched her burning. She wanted more of that, more of his hunger meshing perfectly with hers, not this anger. Because that's what it looked like to her. He was angry and she didn't know why.

When she'd appeared in the doorway and he'd turned from the fire, the look in his eyes flaring silver, she'd thought their earlier tension had been put behind them. Then he'd shocked her with an apology before kissing her and every thought had vanished from her head. She'd thought they were okay, that they'd gone back to what they'd had back in the Cotswolds...

Until he'd pushed himself suddenly away from her.

It didn't make any sense. Had it been her? Had she done something wrong? Had he had second thoughts? What?

'My brother,' she echoed, the words not making any sense to her immediately.

'Yes, Castor Xenakis.' Ares sounded impatient now. 'You need to contact him.'

Rose struggled to process what he was talking about, her head still wrapped around his kiss. Then it penetrated.

Her brother. Whom Ares had found. Castor Xenakis.

She took a breath. 'Oh, I... Yes, I will contact him.'

'Tonight,' Ares said flatly. 'You need to tell him tonight.'

She swallowed, studying his face, trying to see what his issue was and why he was suddenly being so adamant. 'Actually, I thought I'd wait a little bit,' she said carefully. 'I still haven't got my head around—'

'He's been waiting to find you for twenty years. Don't you think he'd want to know that you're alive?'

'Yes, but if he's waited twenty years, he can wait another few hours.' She stared at him. 'Why are you so angry? What is this about, Ares?'

He turned away, lifting his tumbler and draining it. Then he went over to the drinks cabinet and poured himself another measure. He did not look at her.

'You're wrong,' he said after a moment, his attention on his glass. 'I do blame myself.'

'Blame yourself?' she echoed, trying to follow the sudden change in topic. 'Blame your-self for what?'

'Naya's death.' He picked up the glass and stared down into it, as if the liquid contained all the secrets of the universe. 'My father was so proud of the Aristiades line. He always said that we were descended from the great hero Hercules and that's why we were so strong. I shared his pride, thought that the Aristiades name made us better than everyone else. So, when this beautiful daughter of a Russian oli-garch agreed to be my wife, even though I had no money and only a mountain hut for her to live in, I was even prouder. Being a penniless shepherd in the mountains is a hard life, and she was everything I'd never had—softness and beauty and compassion. I loved her to distrac-tion. I was always afraid she might discover one day that she'd made a terrible mistake in mar-rying this poor Greek shepherd boy... Anyway, when Stavros demanded protection money, I refused.' He gave a low, bitter laugh. 'I didn't want her to think that I was a coward, that I was weak. I was an Aristiades and we were the blood of Hercules.'

Rose went cold. He was talking about his wife.

'The night of the fire, I wasn't there,' Ares went on. 'I was helping my father with a ewe having a difficult birth and so they didn't find me until the house was well alight. It was a mountain village—we didn't have a fire engine, only hoses and buckets, so by the time I got there, it was too late. I went in anyway, because I was supposed to be strong enough to protect her, save her, but...' He stopped, then raised his tumbler and downed what was left in there. 'I didn't think the consequences would have been so terrible. She should never have married me. She should have stayed well away.'

The chill had reached her bones now, and was working its way into her heart, that grief she'd felt earlier shredding her emotions once again.

She could see him as a young man, full of youthful pride and arrogance. Yet that wasn't a sin. That was just youth, the feeling of being bulletproof, that nothing bad could ever happen to you because nothing ever had.

It wasn't a feeling she'd ever had. That had been taken from her, just as his had been taken from him. And it had been taken. It wasn't his fault that some awful people had chosen to fire-bomb his house and he shouldn't think that it was. Yet before she could say anything, he went on.

'I was two years recovering from the burns. People kept telling me how lucky I was to be alive, but I didn't feel lucky. I should have died with her. That would have been a just punishment, I think.' He reached for the bottle again and then stopped, his hand dropping as if he'd had second thoughts. He still didn't look at her. 'Afterwards, when I'd healed, I went straight into the Legion, because that's when I decided that if I had to live, I'd do things differently. I'd let my pride and my arrogance, and my anger, blind me, and so I had to get rid of them. They'd led me astray, they'd caused Naya's death, and so they couldn't be trusted.'

Rose's heart ached at the emptiness in his voice, the sheer lack of expression in it. He sounded so bleak it brought tears to her eyes.

'Ares…' she began hoarsely, wanting to say something, to give him some comfort any way she could.

But he gave a sharp shake of his head. 'Let me finish.' He reached for the bottle again and poured himself yet another glass, smaller this time. Then he raised and took a small, careful sip, as if he was rationing it. 'After the Legion, I was adrift for a time. The only thing I had left was Naya's memory. That's what made me build my company. I wanted to do something in her name, create a legacy for her. A company that she would have been proud to be associated with. She became my conscience, my guide. Everything I do, I do for her.' He glanced at her then, his gaze darker than she'd ever seen it. 'My father died a few years back and he made me promise that the Aristiades line would not die with me. I promised him it would not. I also promised Naya when we married that we would have a houseful of children, because she was desperate for them.

'That's why I agreed to marry you, Rose. That's why our marriage was to include children. To fulfil my promise to my father and to Naya. But that's all. If you choose to stay with me, that's all our marriage will ever be, do you understand?'

Her throat felt thick and tight, her vision swimming with tears of pain for him. And from somewhere she dredged up her voice. 'You can't blame yourself for any of that, Ares. It's not your fault—'

'Do you understand?' he repeated over the top of her, his eyes darkening into black in the firelight. 'If you want to stay with me, our marriage will only be for heirs, Rose. For the promises I made. That is all. You cannot mean anything to me. You cannot be important to me. I will give you nothing. All I have left is this—' he glanced down at himself and shook his head '—empty shell, scarred with the reminders of my failure. That is what you will be married to. That is all I can offer.'

Rose felt as if the winter from outside had come in through the windows and was now creeping around her heart, freezing it solid. There was no doubt in those darkened eyes of his, no doubt in his voice either.

'You didn't kill her,' she said hoarsely, because she had to at least attempt to convince him. 'A petrol bomb did. Smoke inhalation did. Not you.'

His gaze didn't waver. 'If I hadn't loved her, I wouldn't have wanted to prove myself to her. If I hadn't been so obsessed with keeping her, I would have paid the money. If I hadn't loved her, she wouldn't have married me in the first place and then she wouldn't have died.'

'Something else might have killed her, you don't know. You can't keep playing "what-ifs" for ever, Ares.' She swallowed past the giant lump that had risen in her throat. 'If I'd stayed put and watched the kittens, if I hadn't seen another kitten in the street and gone to pick it up, perhaps then I wouldn't have been abducted. But I was. Second-guessing won't change that.'

'You're right.' His face was impassive. 'Yet my wife is still dead, and it is still my fault.'

'And it's still my fault I didn't do what I was told. It was my fault I got abducted.'

Finally, the darkness in his eyes shifted, a

flickering silver flame glittering there instead. 'That is not what I said.'

'But it's the same thing, isn't it?' She didn't back down. He had to see what he was saying, he had to. 'You should have paid that money and you didn't, so it's your fault. I should have stayed where I was and I didn't, so that's my fault too.'

A muscle flicked in his jaw. 'You were a child. You were—'

'You were young,' she interrupted. 'You thought nothing could touch you. That's not a crime. Loving someone and wanting to prove yourself to them isn't a crime either. Besides, she loved you too. Or does her choice not matter?'

He only shook his head and said harshly, 'She chose wrong.'

She opened her mouth to argue yet again and then stopped. And looked into his eyes, seeing the silver flames flickering there. Anger, yes, but she could see the grief too. A grief that was still there no matter what he said about getting rid of his emotions.

A grief that unlike his scars had never healed.

You cannot argue with him. You cannot push him. Not about this, not if you care about him.

No, she couldn't, and more, she didn't want to. Because it was true, she did care about him. And it felt as if it was something that had been sitting inside her all along, right from the first moment he'd walked into the room as she was cleaning it. And instead of ignoring her or touching her or even talking to her, he'd sat quietly down in the chair by the fire. He hadn't said a word and she hadn't looked at him, her heart beating so fast with fear, the way it did whenever a guest was around. He hadn't moved or spoken. He'd sat there like a rock, unmoving. And gradually over the course of that first day, she'd begun to realise that he wasn't going to talk to her or reach for her or do any of the things the other guests did. All he was going to do was sit there, watching her. As if he was fascinated and couldn't take his eyes off her.

She'd asked to him to rescue her because he'd felt like someone who would, and she hadn't been disappointed. And over these past few months, as she'd got to know him, she'd come to see that he was a protective man. A man who had kindness in him and generosity, and humour too. A man she could rely on, who would support her and who sparked her passion like no one else. A man who made her feel strong and brave, as if she was the woman she'd always wanted to be.

It wasn't that he didn't feel, that wasn't his problem; she could see that now.

It was that he felt too much; he was still mired in his grief. Living not for himself, but for the woman he'd loved and lost, and who surely wouldn't want to see the agony he was putting himself through.

He stood now beside the fire, the golden light gilding the harsh, scarred lines of his face, somehow making beauty out of the twisted, gouged and roughened flesh. Scars he'd earned trying to save someone he'd loved, because that's the kind of man he was. They weren't signs of the depth of his failure. They were signs of the depth of his love.

And it was in that moment that it hit her, looking at those signs, those terrible, beautiful scars, that she realised she wanted that love too. She wanted his love.

Because it was true the thought that had whispered to her upstairs. She *was* falling for him—or rather, she'd already fallen. And there was no saving her.

She loved him. She loved him completely and utterly without reservation, and while it was probably selfish of her, she wanted him to love her back.

But why should he? You're a silly little girl that didn't do what her big brother told her and got herself abducted? Why should he put aside his grief for the wife he lost for someone like you?

He wouldn't and she would never ask him to. Why make this any harder for him than it needed to be?

He'd lost his wife and he didn't need her wanting things from him. He didn't need her grief for him or her love for him either. What he needed was her body and so that's what she'd give him.

She swallowed, shoved away her own grief and pain, ignored the cold that was threading through her veins. Because she'd made him a promise. She'd told him that at the end of the year she would choose: to stay married to him, to be his wife in all ways, give him the family that he'd wanted or... She would choose to leave.

'If you want children, then you're not going to get them by pushing me away.' She held her arms out to him. 'I've made my choice, Ares. I choose to stay with you and be your wife. So, come and finish what you started.'

He didn't move, his face a mask, his eyes reverting to that dark, stormy ocean with no moonlight on it at all. 'No. My promise to Naya will have to go unfulfilled.'

Her arms dropped, her gut lurching, the cold biting deeper. 'But—'

'You have your brother now, Rose,' he interrupted roughly. 'You should go to him. You don't need me.'

'I don't know my brother.' The words sounded too desperate, but she couldn't stop herself. 'And I want to be with you.'

A flicker of something raw crossed his face, and then it was gone. 'I'm afraid I cannot allow that. Not now.'

It felt like he'd stabbed her, the pain catching her unexpectedly hard deep inside. She stared at him. 'Why not?'

He only stared back, his gaze uncompromising, no give in him at all. A man made of iron, of hard, rigid metal. 'You are free to make a choice, and so am I. And my choice is to annul our marriage. I should never have agreed to it in the first place.'

The knife twisted, making the pain start to radiate like cracks in a broken windowpane, but she ignored it. 'Why? But your promise—'

'Naya is dead.' His eyes glittered blackly. 'And my father is too. They won't know anyway.'

'Ares, don't—'

'Enough.' The word was hard and flat, a sword of iron cutting her off. 'I won't hold you to a marriage that will only cause you distress in the end, and it will, Rose. You deserve more than being the bought wife of a man who only wanted you for your ability to have children. You deserve *better*. You deserve to be loved. That's what marriage means. And that I can never give you.'

There were tears in her eyes, but she forced them back. 'What would you know about what I deserve and what I don't? Perhaps *you* are what I deserve, love or not.'

'Is that what you really want? To be chained for ever to a man who will never love you? Who will never give you the one thing you've wanted all your life—and you have wanted it, little maid, don't deny it. How is that any different to being Vasiliev's prisoner?'

The knife inside her twisted a little more, a little deeper. She'd had years of loneliness, years of unhappiness. Years of having nothing and no one but Athena, and yes, he was right. She wanted more than that.

She *did* want love. But the love she wanted was his.

She felt as if she was falling into pieces inside, but she decided she wasn't going to beg. She wouldn't plead or weep either. She would stand tall and strong and tell him that she loved him, because regardless of what he could give her, she wanted to give this to him.

She was a warrior and there was a strength inside her, a steel, and now she knew where that steel came from. It came from love. Her love for him.

'I love you,' she said, swallowing her tears and reaching for the fierce part of her. 'Doesn't that make any difference at all?'

He went very still, his gaze focusing on her, something bright glittering there. Then abruptly he looked down at the vodka bottle on the bar instead. 'No. It only makes me more certain that dissolving this marriage is the right thing to do. I will not be your jailer, Rose. I want you to be free.'

She blinked hard against the prickling tears. 'But how can I be free when you aren't? And you're not, Ares. You're letting your grief trap you, can't you see that?'

'I chose my cage. You did not choose yours.'

'But what if I want to? Don't I have a right to choose my own?'

The line of his powerful shoulders radiated tension, his ruined profile harder than stone. He didn't look at her. 'You can. But I'm not going to be the one to close the cage door.' The muscle in his jaw twitched again, his expression hardening. 'I'm going send for the helicopter. There is no need for me to stay here any longer. You, however, may stay as long as you wish.'

Then abruptly he turned away and strode from the room before she could speak.

CHAPTER TEN

Spring

ARES NORMALLY LOVED spring in the mountains of his Greek homeland. He would often allow himself a week in his house there, close to the village where he'd grown up. Where the air was clean and fresh, the sky was deep blue and the cold of winter was fading, yet the baking heat of summer hadn't yet had a chance to settle in.

His house was more of a castle, perched on the side of one of the mountains near his old village. It had been built in medieval times, and he'd had it refurbished at huge expense, the only exceptions he made for modernity being a fast satellite internet connection, power and running water.

Mainly, though, he liked it because it was isolated and there was no one to bother him. Plus, being in the mountains, near the place where he'd been born, was a good reminder of his own failures.

Four weeks after he'd left Rose in Iceland, he'd sent her through divorce papers. She might have chosen to stay married to him, but he couldn't hold her to it. Because regardless of what she'd said about choosing her own cage, about being in love with him, well… What did she know about love? She might know what a cage was, he'd let her have that, but love? No, she had no idea.

He did, though. Love blinded you. It betrayed you. It gouged out your heart and burned it to ashes and left you with nothing. He couldn't trust it, never again. Rose hadn't learned those lessons yet, and with any luck, she never would.

What she deserved was all the love, all the happiness. She deserved everything she wanted, but that wasn't him.

Telling her that in the living room of the lodge in Iceland had hurt her, he knew. And the look on her face, the pain he'd seen in her big golden eyes, had hurt something inside him too. But he was used to pain so he ignored it. Besides, he couldn't see another way.

She loved him and he didn't love her, and he never would. He couldn't allow himself to. The only love he'd ever trusted was Naya's. He couldn't trust his own.

Rose would heal in time—she was nothing if not resilient—and then she'd be free to find someone else who would love her the way he couldn't.

That thought made him want to roar in denial, but he ignored that too, shoving it to one side as he walked in the castle olive grove the morning after he'd arrived. His gardener had some queries about some of the trees and talking about that was an excellent distraction from the subject of Rose.

He had to stop thinking about her. He had to.

Ares had paused beneath a particular tree, his gardener pointing at something on the branches, when one of Ares's assistants came hurrying over the green lawn with news.

Apparently, so his assistant said, his wife was not only *not* going to sign the divorce papers, but she was also never going to sign them, and if Ares didn't like that, he could stick them in an anatomically incorrect and very painful place.

Ares stood beneath the olive tree as his assistant relayed Rose's response, aware of an intense fury gathering inside him. A fury in defiance of his own self-control and out of all proportion to her refusal. Fury that she was making this harder than it needed to be, and how she appeared not to have listened to a word he'd said.

He'd told her he would never give her what she needed. Didn't she want to be free?

Obviously, she hadn't been listening, which meant they were going to need to have another little chat. A phone call wasn't enough, and he definitely wasn't going to email her. No, he needed to see her in person.

He didn't ask himself why it was so important she understand, not when he'd been telling himself all this time that he wasn't supposed to care. And he didn't question the need to leave Greece immediately when he'd only just arrived.

He left the grove, took the helicopter back to Athens where he kept the jet, had it fuelled and ready to leave for Paris within the hour. And as the jet powered its way across Europe, he went over in his head again and again what he was going to say to her.

She had to sign those divorce papers. He couldn't keep her. He wouldn't.

Paris in spring was beautiful, but Ares took no notice, heading straight to the cafe by the Seine, where Rose worked. It was just on closing time and most of the customers had left already, but Ares wasn't in any mood to wait.

He had with him a couple of security staff who discreetly got rid of the last two customers, then stationed themselves outside the cafe door. Rose was inside; he could see her through the windows, standing beside the counter and looking down at something.

And he had to take a slow, silent breath as everything drew tight inside him, the fury that had sustained him all the way from Greece turning into something hotter and more demanding.

He tried to shove it away as he pushed open the door and stepped inside, tried to ignore it as the door closed behind him, but as Rose turned her attention to the door, and those big golden eyes of hers met his, it erupted inside him like a volcano.

He froze, his control hanging by a thread, knowing that even moving one muscle would annihilate that thread and he would be closing the distance between them and dragging her into his arms.

You will never let her go.

He couldn't do that. He wouldn't.

Rose's eyes widened, an expression of shock crossing her lovely features, to be followed by one of pure joy, as if seeing him had been the best thing to have ever happened to her in her entire life. Then just as quickly as it had appeared, the joy faded into something harder, more determined, and her chin lifted, her spine straightening.

The warrior ready for battle.

Instantly he wanted to cross the space be-

tween them and bring that battle right to her.
Match her and master her and make her his.

But he closed his hands into fists and stayed
where he was instead.

'Why did you not sign those documents?' he
demanded, getting straight to the point. 'You
need to be free, Rose. You do not need to be
married to me any more.'

'And I told you that I don't want to be free,
remember?' she snapped straight back. 'Not of
you.'

'It's been a month. You really still—'

'Nothing has changed.' She looked so fierce
as she took a step towards him. '*Nothing.* I told
you I wanted to choose my own cage and I
have.'

Frustration curled inside him, made more
acute by the feeling rushing through him, the
powerful need to get close to her, have nothing
between them. 'I can't give you what you want.
I told you that. Not to you and not to any children we have—'

'What do you want, Ares?'

'What?' The question was so out of left field
he couldn't process it. 'What do you mean what
do I want?'

'I mean, what do *you* want?'

'The promise I made to Naya—'

'No. What do *you* want for *yourself*?'

He stared at her, the words not making any sense for a moment. Then they did and his brain instantly provided the answer.

Her. You want her.

It felt like someone had put their fingers around his throat and was squeezing hard, choking the breath from his body.

She only looked at him, all the ferocity gathering into a bright, hot, burning look that rooted him to the spot.

You know why you're here. Why you flew across a continent to get to her. And it's not to sign divorce papers.

It was that feeling inside him, the one he didn't want to examine. The one he didn't want to feel, not again. Because he'd felt it before. He'd felt it with Naya. The same and yet different this time, because it was Rose standing in front of him.

Rose, who wasn't afraid of him. Who matched him will for will. Who laughed with him and fought with him, and in the end trusted him. Rose, who hadn't let any of the experiences she'd gone through grind her into dust, but who'd emerged victorious. Rose, whose courage shocked him and who'd grasped what life had given her and had bent it to her will.

Rose, who touched his scars as if they were more than reminders of his failure.

Rose, whom he knew now he'd fallen in love with despite every part of him trying to resist.

Rose, who'd restarted his dead heart and now it was beating and beating for her alone.

'You,' Ares said, the words coming out of him harsh and raw. 'I want you. I want to keep you. I want you to be my wife for ever. But I can't. Love lies. It cannot be trusted. And my love will kill you just as surely as it killed Naya.'

It had taken all of Rose's considerable will not to cross the distance between them and fling herself into his arms the moment Ares had stepped through the door and into the cafe.

She'd never expected him to come to Paris for her, not even once.

The past month had been a busy one, though he'd never been far from her thoughts. She'd finally gathered her courage to make contact with the brother she'd thought she'd lost, and their reunion had both torn her apart and then put her back together again.

Castor had welcomed her with open arms, and she'd got to meet his lovely wife, Glory, and their son, her nephew. It had been so bittersweet, giving her back parts of herself she'd thought she'd lost for ever. Yet one part was still missing. The part of herself she'd given away.

Her heart.

She'd stayed for a couple of weeks in that lodge in Iceland after Ares had left, not knowing what to do. Whether to go to him and beg to be taken back or go to Paris and try to forget he ever existed.

Except she couldn't do either of those things. Firstly, even if she'd wanted to beg him to, she suspected he wouldn't take her back, and secondly, she was never going to forget him. She was never going to want another man. It was only and always ever going to be him.

Yet she couldn't let him be alone either. She had a new-found family in Castor and Glory now, but who did he have? No one. He was alone with only that lonely legacy of a company, and she hated that thought more than anything in the world.

So, when the divorce papers had come through, she'd simply refused to sign them, because she'd wanted him to know that she wasn't going to let him go so easily.

She'd just never thought he'd come all the way over here to confront her.

But that meant something, didn't it?

She could see it now as he stood by the door, so tall and powerful and so beautifully scarred. The depths of his love worn proud for the world to see.

'Your love didn't kill Naya,' she said quietly.

'It didn't, Ares. Your love made you go into a burning building for her, made you risk your life for her. Your love built a company in her memory, a company that helps people the world over. You didn't fail her. She was taken from you, that's the tragedy.' She took a soft, shaky breath. 'But you can't go on letting a memory be your own reason for living. And you can't go on living in your grief.'

His eyes were completely dark, his big, muscled body tense as a coiled spring. 'That is not—'

'You were badly hurt. And you're afraid. But you're lonely too, Ares. You need someone.' She stared at him, willing him to see the love that was burning in her eyes, the love she had for him. 'Naya loved you and she would want happiness for you, not this…half-life you're living now. She would look at the scars on your face and see how deeply you loved her, not how badly you failed her.'

His expression twisted, a muscle in his jaw flicking. 'How could you possibly know that? You didn't know her.'

'No, but we both love you.' She was very calm all of a sudden, trusting the feeling inside her. 'And that's what I want for you. And I think that's what she'd want for you too.'

Agony glittered in his eyes, and grief, and

anger. So many different emotions, all the ones he'd been locking inside himself that he was finally now showing to her.

And she couldn't stay where she was any longer.

She stepped away from the counter and crossed the distance between them, and he didn't move, watching her as she came. And when she was right in front of him, she lifted her hands and placed them lightly on his chest, looking up into his beautiful, ruined face.

'These are love, Ares.' She reached up and touched him, tracing the lines of his scars. 'These are all love. Can you feel it?'

'Little maid,' he said hoarsely, his rasping voice vibrating with something powerful. 'Little maid…' He turned his head into her hand, watching her as if he couldn't drag his gaze away. 'When Naya died…part of me died too. And I don't know… I don't know if I can do this again with you.'

'I understand. After what you lost…' She touched his hard mouth, looked up into his eyes. 'It must be frightening to risk your heart again. And I know I haven't lost what you have, but… I'm scared too. Yet all I can think is why shouldn't we both get what we want? Don't we deserve it? Don't we deserve to be happy?'

He made a harsh sound. 'Do you really want

this? Do you really want to be tied to someone like me? I don't know if what I have to give you will ever be enough. I'm scarred and broken, and…'

'Still grieving,' she finished and smiled. 'You may be scarred, but you're not broken, Ares. You're kind and protective, and whether you like it or not, you're caring. And there is no time limit on grief.' Her fingertips drifted to trace the line of his bottom lip. 'We can work it out between us.'

'Rose…' The look in his eyes had lightened, the moon coming out from behind the clouds and shining on a green sea. Then he took her hand and pressed a kiss to her palm. 'How can I divorce you when I think I'm in love with you?'

'Are you?' Her chest was tight with the pressure of everything she felt for him, the huge, complicated feeling that had tied itself into a knot behind her ribs. But it was a good pressure and it felt right. As if now she was finally whole. 'You can't divorce me. I won't let you.'

Abruptly the look on his face changed, and she was being pulled against his hard, powerful body and he was bending his head, his mouth covering hers in a kiss that consumed the entire world.

'No, little maid,' Ares murmured against her mouth. '*This* is love.'

And he spent the rest of his life proving it to her.

EPILOGUE

ARES LOUNGED ON a blanket in the olive grove just below his castle in Greece, keeping a watchful eye on his son, Niko. The boy had just learned to crawl, and Ares could already tell he was going to be the kind of child who got into everything and caused havoc for his parents.

He couldn't wait.

Not far away, his little maid was playing with her nephew and twin nieces while her brother, Castor, looked on. He and Glory were visiting, and Ares found he quite enjoyed their company, even though he had a healthy disdain for men from the islands, which Castor was. Glory, however, was a delight, and it was true that Castor loved his sister very much, which was a point in his favour. As Rose loved him.

But Castor didn't love her as much as Ares did.

He'd sold his company, and after much discussion with Rose, they'd both decided to invest the money in the mountain villages of his homeland, giving back to many of the poorer communities. Naya would have liked that, he was certain.

Rose had also taken some of his money and, along with Castor, had founded an organisation dedicated to helping the victims of human trafficking. She was very, very good at it, and a fierce advocate.

But what was most important was that she was happy, and he knew because she told him so every day. Just as he told her the same thing. And he was. He'd never thought he would be again, never thought he would have deserved it, but Rose had shown him that he did. She had given him the courage to realise that despite all his talk of legacies and memorials, he'd been doing exactly what she'd accused him of: living in his grief. Using it to keep himself protected, because he knew grief. It was familiar. It was safe. But loving again wasn't, especially loving someone different. Loving Rose was like exploring an undiscovered country: it definitely wasn't safe. There were threats everywhere, and yet also such beauty. Such joy. Such happiness.

He didn't regret a moment of it.

Niko had reached his knee and gripped it

with chubby fists, pulling himself up onto his feet for the first time, and grinning madly at his father.

And Ares felt his heart grow bigger, beating strong and hard behind his ribs.

He smiled at his son, and when he looked over at Rose to draw her attention to Niko's brilliance, he found her already looking back, her golden eyes full of light.

She smiled, glowing in the late summer afternoon, the slight breeze blowing the red dress she wore against her figure, the little bump that was their second child already visible.

His heart beat stronger, harder.

She'd restarted that heart again, his little maid.

She'd made it beat.

And every beat was love.

* * * * *